The Unprize

Linda Ruth Brooks

A copy of this book can be found in the National Library of Australia

Cover Design; Linda Brooks

ISBN-978-0-6481902-0-2

Fiction/Contemporary women

The Unprize is a work of fiction. Any similarity between the characters in this book and real people, living or dead, is coincidental.

This book, and others by Linda Ruth Brooks, can be found at online bookstores and other retail outlets.

Chapter 1

'Oh wow! The world just exploded in a riot of colour and...What?' Chelsea screamed into the phone. 'I'm at the Harbour Bridge and a million tonnes of fireworks just went off. I can't hear you, but that's probably because I'm *now deaf!*'

It was New Year's Eve. The noisy countdown to the New Year had just finished and the annual fireworks display had begun, lighting up the indigo sky. Chelsea was at the Opera House with a camera crew. There was a lull between the fireworks, then chuckling. Chelsea moaned as she realised her voice had carried to the film and stage crew.

'You did it again, didn't you!' screeched Leisa. She found Chelsea's bolshie attitude and antics endlessly entertaining.

'Did what?' complained Chelsea.

'You put your foot in it again, didn't you? I wish I was there to see the looks on everyone's faces,' Leisa snorted, trying to control her laughter.

That was the trouble with best friends; they knew you too well, thought Chelsea. If anyone was aware of her tendency to say the wrong thing at the wrong time, it was Leisa.

'What are you doing anyway?' said Chelsea in mock offense, ignoring the guffaws of the film crew. 'You're supposed to be in labour. Hasn't my godchild arrived yet? You'd better get a move on. I am not going to fill in for you forever you know, this is your job I am slaving over down here.

Chelsea changed the mobile phone to her other ear as she struggled to catch Leisa's words. Leisa was gabbling on about some competition.

'Are you okay?' Chelsea questioned in the next lull, her voice softening.

The fireworks started again and even though Chelsea put her finger in her ear and put her head in the corner she couldn't hear Leisa and after giving the phone a fierce stare she rammed a nail-chewed finger on the disconnect button and slammed it into her apron pocket.

The things you do for your best friend. She was down at Darling Harbour because she had been dragged into the promotion of Leisa's catering business, 'Cooking up a Storm'.

The colourful New Year's celebration had been the backdrop for a promotion photo shoot. The photos would be made into a calendar featuring a dish from Leisa's catering menu for each month. One of the models had been sick and Chelsea had to fill in at the last minute. She consoled herself that she was merely a prop and with any luck would be unrecognizable with the dramatic makeup and the shoulder length Cleopatra style wig that all the models had worn. Her friends at the preschool would have a field day if they recognized her posing for the calendar.

All that had been left for her to do was pack the food and the bohemian crystal they had used for the shoot. Unlike the models her work was not over and if the garbled message from Leisa meant what she thought it did, she would be stuck here longer.

'Another competition,' moaned Chelsea to herself. Leisa had asked her to stay a 'few more minutes' to hear the prize announced for her latest competition entry.

Leisa had become a competition junkie since becoming pregnant.

'Forced bed rest will do that to a girl,' an unrepentant Leisa had explained.

She had done very well out of it. This time she had entered the 'Daydream about Soap' competition. The winner would be announced after the fireworks. The competition was a promotion for the soap opera that was filmed in Surfer's Paradise called 'Daydream Island'. Even though there was a real island called Daydream Island the series was filmed in Surfer's Paradise on the Gold Coast. Chelsea hated the soap with a vengeance. Overacted and deliberately schmaltzy, it was her idea of torture.

Leisa had watched it religiously in hospital. She had acquired two addictions while in hospital for pre-eclampsia. Entering competitions in celebrity magazines and watching the soap. Chelsea had been delighted for Leisa's anxieties to be replaced by the 'aimless nonsense' of other peoples' lives.

Leisa had been inundated with magazines from caring friends. It would be a crying shame not to devour them. Chelsea had called it a 'low-cal craving'. Chelsea thought it was marvellous. Not only had Leisa won a swag load of prizes that she was more than happy to share but because it took Leisa's mind off this pregnancy and the worry that came with it. Leisa had miscarried early in the marriage and Chelsea had been concerned for her lifelong friend. Leisa had waited a long time to find love again and Mike was a gem. This pregnancy had been an added blessing even though it had meant extended time in hospital over the last six weeks.

Hopefully, she would be able to leave as soon as the winner was announced. Leisa had been adamant that she wait for the announcement. The competition entry was in her name apparently. Chelsea had dictated some over-the-top nonsense to Leisa that was intended to satirize the show. She consoled herself that the promoters were hardly likely to look favourably on her entry.

Frankly, she didn't want to win. She wouldn't mind a holiday at Surfer's and the accompanying spending money, but part of the prize was a walk-on role on the 'soap'. Chelsea was horrified at that thought. Worse still, she vaguely remembered Leisa saying that the prize also included a chance to meet the cast and stay in their hotel.

Chelsea couldn't recall what she had dictated to Leisa. At the time Chelsea had been helping Mike prepare dinner for the Christmas Party for his building company. Leisa had been ensconced in a big arm chair with her swollen feet on the ottoman. Mike had joked that he might as well take a wall out and join the lounge room to the kitchen because with Leisa on enforced rest he'd had to move half the house into the kitchen. Leisa had thrown a tea towel at him. She kept up the rapid fire instructions to both of them while filling in the entry form.

'I hope this 'low-cal craving' ends with the pregnancy,' Mike had moaned.

'I wouldn't hold my breath if I was you,' muttered Chelsea in return.

'Don't talk about me as if I'm not here, you two,' said Leisa as her sharpened pencil prodded the magazine impatiently. 'Come on Chelsea, you're the writer, spill.'

Shaking herself from the reverie Chelsea surveyed the set. It was no use thinking about the competition. Nothing was going to help her remember the entry.

She didn't notice a man who had watched her all evening from the comfort of a faded deck chair. The tall, dark man was sitting just behind the glare of the lights. Jack Devon narrowed his eyes to follow the movements of the woman who had entertained him on this long night where he had expected to face terminal boredom.

From the minute she had stepped out with her micro mini skirt under that ridiculously large apron and that sassy smile on her face he had been enchanted. She had tripped over the wires, she had sworn softly when she had been unable to light the candle for the fondue for her scene. She had lost her glasses after putting them on and off to read the cue card that held the instructions for the shoot.

She had gabbed all through her segment of the photo shoot to the riotous enjoyment of the whole crew. Jack guessed that she had no concept of 'still' photography, or still anything for that matter. She was a refreshing delight, more delectable than the menu.

He suspected that she was not a professional model, not only because she was curvier than the other women, but she had self-deprecating candour. He found her lack of pretence charming. No model would make a circus out of using a pair of glasses the way Chelsea had done.

The other models had vamped it up on cue with their seductive pouts and their tiny aprons had been token efforts. Chelsea had arrived with her silky black Cleopatra style wig askew and an apron ten times the size of the other girls. It was the same style as the other models' aprons with bold white lettering displaying, 'Cooking up a Storm' but she obviously preferred the functional apron rather than the skimpy ones the other girls wore. He found her self-consciousness endearing.

However the real clue had been her constant chattering compared to the sultry silence of the others. She had been unashamedly hilarious. He loved a woman who didn't take herself too seriously.

She certainly had comic timing; the bedroom scene with the

Arabian nights setting she had just pulled off was nothing short of genius. Totally unrehearsed and natural. He smiled again as he relaxed back in the chair with his hands behind his head. The others girls had pulsed with sexuality but Chelsea had hammed it up and had everyone howling.

She had been nervous initially when she came on but when the candle wouldn't light she had purred, 'Cooking up a storm in the bedroom takes a bit longer when the fire has gone out.' She had leant in a mock seductive pose on the red satin sheets with a rose between her teeth and slipped off the bed, falling with her legs inelegantly in the air.

She looked like a modern day Cleopatra with those dramatic eyes and the fall of dark shiny hair that she blew out of her face. Lucille Ball had nothing on this one. She had walked around the fondue set that was perched on the bed and rambled on to the stage hand who had stepped up to the candle to light it with a cigarette lighter.

'Of course, a storm in the bedroom is so much better with a man to light the fire.' She had purred and batted her eyes theatrically, pretending to lose one of her false eyelashes. The stage hand had blushed. When the lighter failed to work Chelsea had put her hands on her hips and deadpanned in a deep Mae West voice, 'Get a blow torch, honey.'

Jack had been doubled over with tears streaming down his eyes. He suspected that the green eyed minx couldn't see the reaction of the crew and doubted that she knew that the whole segment had been filmed by the Channel 7 news crew that was roaming the Quay. They had stumbled onto the set in their wandering quest for the colour and flavour of the various entertainments of the night. If Jack knew anything her performance was sheer gold. What he would pay to get a copy of that clip. He'd bet anything that she hadn't noticed the extra cameras.

He was right. Chelsea hadn't noticed because she didn't know the difference between a still photo shoot and a taped segment. The cameras all looked the same to her. She was a 'ring in'.

Chelsea pulled her mobile phone out of the apron pocket. She returned it after a quick glance for messages. It was no use ringing Leisa or Mike while the fireworks continued to part the night air with their staccato popping.

A low rumbling sound combined with a tightening of her stomach made Chelsea realise that she was starving. Food, God that was why she was becoming tetchy. She looked around in despair. Most of the food that had been used for the photo shoot was fake. Of course; it would be.

Eyeing the models as they negligently draped themselves over the opera house steps she decided they would be no use to ask about nourishment of any kind. She hadn't seen them put anything in their pouty mouths except cigarettes.

Perhaps they didn't want to be caught with spinach between their teeth for the photos. Chelsea chuckled. As if *that* could happen. The stick thin models had constantly checked their appearance in more mirrors than Chelsea had even seen in the House of Mirrors at Luna Park. Even that hadn't satisfied the girls as they had frequently questioned each other in frantic voices about their hair or makeup.

She would have to have a word with Leisa about more realistic models. These girls looked as if they hadn't seen the inside of a kitchen, much less eaten in one. She smiled softly as she thought of a calendar with size 16 girls modelling for a catering calendar—now that would be believable! Even better if they had actually been eating in the photos. Her imagination was fired as she thought of sticky chocolate sauce travelling towards glorious real cleavage.

Food, she thought, find food; now! Then she remembered the salad platter that had been laid out for the models on a tiny table under the carnival umbrella near their dressing tent. Surely there would be something there. She giggled as the thought struck her that near the models tent would have to be the safest place to keep food. It was probably untouched.

She tripped over the long legs of a man sitting just inside the dressing tent. The models had vacated, leaving their clothes for the unseen assistants to clear. Jack had moved from the busy boardwalk to get some peace from the noisy throng. His face was shadowed. A hot pink feather boa was restlessly flapping beside him. Probably a groupie hoping to perv on the models, Chelsea mused, although those shoes looked like they had cost a fortune.

Without glancing in the direction of 'the feet' she muttered something that sounded remotely like a disgruntled apology. She quickly assessed him as one of the bored executives who managed to get through the endless obligatory year-end social events with a mixture of cocaine and booze. Maybe he was in a coma. He hadn't even moved when she tripped over his feet. Served him right.

Dismissing all thought of him she found the table under the colourful umbrella. Her heart sank to her now-cramped stomach as she saw how little food was left.

Jack's mouth twitched in sheer enjoyment as he watched Chelsea circle the food table; her expressive eyes full of disappointment. Folding his elegant hands behind his head he continued to follow her every move with fascinated amusement. This was better than pay TV. He stayed still and silent, not wishing to disturb the naturalness of her movements. She combined an unpretentious air with an innate grace that was indefinable. She was like a book that he wanted to read. A book with a great opening line that made you impatient to turn the page; hungry for more.

'I'd kill for a sandwich,' Chelsea said loudly to herself. There was a guffaw from the stage crew. She ignored them. She had long ago embraced the fact that she spoke some of her inner thoughts out loud. If anyone had been brave enough to point out that it was the first sign of madness she had quietly informed them that it was the only truly effective way to have intelligent conversation whenever she liked.

'This is do-able,' she muttered as she lay several lettuce leaves on top of each other and then put some crackers, dip, cheese, pesto and several cherry tomatoes on top and then rolled the whole lot into something vaguely resembling a wrap. It was an ungainly, lumpy wrap but Chelsea's eyes rolled in delight as she attacked it with obvious gusto. She wiped the juice from the side of her mouth and sucked her fingers with relish. Jack's hands clasped tighter behind his head. God, she was sexy.

'What do you call that?' said one of the stage construction crew, eyeing her concoction suspiciously. He was also casting a hungry eye over Chelsea's curvy body. As usual she was oblivious.

'Groucho Marx would have known,' she responded; eyes twinkling. She wiggled her top lip in true Marx fashion and wagged the wrap like a cigar, in a flawless caricature of Groucho of the famed Marx Brothers.

'You're a scream, Cleopatra,' chortled the muscular workman.

Chelsea had already turned away to pack up the rest of the food. She didn't notice the workman's lingering look as he shrugged his shoulders. His interest was obvious but Chelsea was completely unaware. Not that she would have paid him much attention any other time. He wasn't her type. Even though he resembled a popular rugby star Chelsea wasn't into nuggetty macho men. That was more Leisa's style. Chelsea had lost count of the times she heard about Mike's powerful thighs.

Her appetite sated, Chelsea realised it was time to clean up. She called out to the two teenage boys who had been doing work experience with the catering business. It was time to deflect them from staring at the size 0 models and get them working. They were good kids who wanted to study hospitality at the local tech college but they needed constant goading. One of the boys, who Chelsea only knew as Gecko, yelled to his father to open the van so they could pack the gear away. All of the expensive glassware had already been packed fastidiously by Bethany, Leisa's assistant, so all that remained was the filling of the garbage bags with the leftover food, disposable plates and champagne flutes.

Chelsea raised her hand to wrench the wig from her head when she saw that the models had thrown their plastic glasses on the Opera House steps. With an exasperated sigh she headed over to them trailing a large black plastic bag. Honestly, would it kill them to bend down to pick up a few glasses! Apparently they could spend hours on the treadmill and the Stairmaster at the Gym where they religiously burned calories but couldn't be bothered moving a muscle to save work for someone else.

Before adding the garbage bag to the growing pile of rubbish Chelsea tore the wig from her head to reveal a lush head of caramel curls. Jack had thought she looked stunning with sleek black hair but with the rich rampant spirals in chestnut and caramel she was a vibrant vision.

I've always been partial to caramel, thought Jack as he continued to admire the curve of Chelsea's derriere as she haphazardly threw food into the rubbish bin and then deftly wrapped the crystal in butchers' paper placing it into the boxes marked with the catering firm logo. He took a mental note of the phone number. This vixen must work for the catering firm given the familiarity she had with the catering equipment. Or perhaps she worked in PR. He would have to try and wrangle an introduction. Relaxing back, he stretched his long legs now thoroughly cramped from the canvas deck chair. There was a crack as he hit the pavement with a thud, the timber frame of the chair in ludicrous pieces beneath him.

Chelsea heard the noise and looked up to see lanky limbs

everywhere. Someone had fallen just behind the lights that were being packed away by the photographer. Probably some drunken reveller. She rushed over to help but by the time she got there Jack was back on his feet massaging a bruised elbow that had connected with the hard cement.

Seizing his opportunity he held out a hand and said, 'Devon, I'm Devon.' He moaned at his awkwardness. Chelsea grabbed his arm and was checking it out. Jack flushed with embarrassment, she had thought he was complaining about his arm when all he had wanted to do was to fold his hand around the fingers that were now expertly exploring his forearm.

'Devon? Are you still talking to your mother after being named after a ham sandwich?' she queried as she dropped his arm with a murmured, 'You'll live, no blood loss.'

'My mother's dead,' muttered Jack hating himself more every minute for his ineptitude with this entrancing creature. He was acting like a tongue tied teenager.

'Oh damn, I'm sorry, I've done it again, terminal foot and mouth disease,' said Chelsea putting her hand sympathetically on his arm.

'Never mind...' Jack began but one of the other catering staff had called out to Chelsea and was asking for instructions on where to put the boxes she had neatly packed. And she was gone. He didn't even know her name. It obviously wasn't Cleopatra.

Chapter 2

Honestly, thought Chelsea these damn fireworks were going on forever. Usually she loved the fireworks display that was an integral part of the annual New Year's Eve celebrations at the Harbour but waiting for Leisa to deliver the baby was beginning to wear on her nerves. Leisa and Mike were like a second family to Chelsea. Her father had died several years ago and her mother was in a Nursing Home back in Tamworth. Her twin brothers Mitchell and Terry now lived in the old family homestead with its ten acre property in Tamworth. Her sister Alicia was living in Indonesia with her husband Lance. The boys hardly ever came to 'the big smoke' and Chelsea hadn't seen Alicia for two years.

Their father had been a shearer's cook and the family had lived a nomadic life following him around as he went from property to property chasing whatever seasonal work he could find. Alicia had taken after their father and loved to travel and try anything new but the boys had settled down as soon as they turned 18 and became mechanics. They both worked for a wealthy landowner, maintaining his tractors and machinery. They were saving to open their own mechanic workshop in town.

Chelsea missed her family even though they stayed in touch by phone. Things weren't the same since their mother Iris had succumbed to Alzheimer's at 49. She had been the glue that held them together, especially since their father had deserted them, failing to send for the family after finding yet another remote position. He had decided the family was tying him down. He returned often bearing expensive gifts and acting as if he had never been away, much to Alicia's disgust and anger but Chelsea had accepted his comings and goings as natural. There hadn't been much change in the time they spent with him anyway and at long last the family had been able to stay in one place.

The security of belonging somewhere was what Chelsea had longed for ever since those happy childhood years when she had lived next door to Leisa in Tamworth. Her father had worked as a short order chef for one of the restaurants in town. The family had lived in the home of Iris's mother and although Chelsea's father had chafed at living with his mother-in-law Chelsea had loved everything about their time there.

Chelsea had relished the comforts of home and regular schooling and had cried bitterly when they moved because of their father's itchy feet and desire to take up the life of the shearer's cook. He had been full of good cheer and promises that his new job would give him more time with the family along with more money. He said that with the seasonal work they would be able to have long summer holidays at the beach where he would teach them all to swim and snorkel. Holidays that never eventuated with the excuses offered being endless.

His perennial optimism and charm had seen him through life. He had been an army chef before his marriage to Iris and Alicia said that he had never put down roots until he died. Alicia was bitter enough for all of them even though she was the one most like him. She often accused Chelsea of being in denial about their father but Chelsea thought she was fully aware of their father's vagabond nature and his shallow family commitment. She just didn't like to dwell on the negatives. She had wanted to forget and move on.

What Chelsea was in denial about was the extent that his defection had affected her. She had never committed herself to a man until just last year. Her world had come crashing down when she had finally agreed to let Jeff move some of his belongings into her flat.

She had been devastated by the depth of the sense of betrayal she experienced when she found out that he was married. She had been expecting the removal van with his belongings to arrive and had been shocked to face an irate woman who was delivering his property in an altogether different fashion; by throwing them in the front yard

When his wife Antonia had told her soggy tale and realised that Chelsea wasn't the husband stealing bitch from hell but just another victim she had wailed her way through a bottle of Chelsea's best chardonnay, incidentally one Jeff had bought and put on ice to celebrate their new life together. It had been fitting somehow to watch his wife work her way aggressively through the bottle until she had melted into a pitiful heap of tears on Chelsea's kitchen table.

Chelsea had gone cold at the thought of the pain that would be inflicted on Jeff's three children when his wife had showed her their trusting faces shining out of their recent school photos. She should have known that Jeff's talk about part time living arrangements were suspect but it had suited her lack of trust and independence. She couldn't believe that she had fallen for a man like her father.

Her father had another woman, Joy, hidden away for over a year before any of them realised the real reason for their father's defection. When she found, out a teenaged Alicia had gone to Joy's house and had thrown rocks on her house screaming for their father to show his lying cheating face. Alicia had been questioned by the police who had been called out by neighbours. Joy had not pressed charges when she saw Alicia's proud angry face streaked with mascara stained tears but the humiliation and shame stayed with Alicia.

Chelsea had not felt any anger towards her father and felt no malice towards Joy. She told herself she felt nothing at all. But sitting across from Jeff's pretty young wife had brought the long buried memories home to her again and her rage at Jeff's actions were ignited, especially when she realised that Antonia was 'my mate Tony' that Jeff had spoken to on the phone when he had been with her. She cooled down quite quickly when she had seen Antonia's over-bright eyes as she suggested that they both take his things and throw them off the Gap, the high cliff over Sydney Harbour that was notorious as a suicide destination.

She had phoned Antonia's sister who had come promptly and taken her wailing sibling home to her place and arranged to pick Antonia and Jeff's children up from school. A sozzled Antonia had promised undying friendship and sisterhood with Chelsea as her voluptuous raven haired sister had hauled her into the car to talk sense into her.

Chelsea had slumped in relief in her over-stuffed lounge chair as Antonia had waved from her sister's sleek black BMW. There had been no explanation necessary to Jeff because when he arrived later Antonia's VW Golf was still sitting in the driveway and his clothes were still strewn over Chelsea's front lawn. 'A picture paints a thousand words', was all Chelsea had to say as she put her hand out for the return of her key, and her life.

The harbour bridge lit up with hot pink flashes of light following by whistling streaks of gold that made the curved bridge look like a giant tiara. It really was beautiful, Chelsea thought. She would have enjoyed it any other time. She realised that the fireworks must be coming to an end as the workers were setting up the microphones on the small makeshift podium near. The band was getting ready to sing 'You Always' the theme song from 'Daydream Island'. As far as Chelsea was concerned the word always didn't belong in a theme song for a soap opera where the players changed partners more often than they changed their underwear. 'Always' was a pretty big ask at the best of times in Chelsea's experience.

She was glad she had changed out of the hot stuffy wig and that ridiculous mini skirt; she was much more comfortable in her knee length white overalls with cross over straps. She had pinned her shoulder length caramel curls high on her head with a huge stray paper clip and she impatiently tapped the clipboard that held Leisa's detailed instructions for the evening.

The man who had fallen off his chair before was standing on the podium straightening his hastily added tie and buttoning the suit coat that he had also just thrown on. Well, he obviously wasn't drunk, Chelsea thought as she watched his quick confident movements. He must be one of the competition officials or an actor from 'Daydream Island'. He certainly had the looks for it she thought as she eyed his slim build and the lush dark hair that he was dragging long elegant fingers through. He looked bored, as if he wanted to be anywhere but here. He looked over the heads of everyone and she assessed him as insufferably arrogant. She knew the type; another Jeff.

Shock rifled through her as she heard the perky blonde PR woman who had been bustling around for hours call out her name straight after the loud phrase—'the winner is...' Oh damn, she thought as the camera panned the crowd. Pasting a bright smile on her face she headed for podium. She might as well get this over with. She dragged her tired feet into action and realised as she started up the steps of the podium that she was beginning to get a blister on her left heel from the dratted high heels. Never mind, only a few more minutes and it would all be over.

The handsome hunk who was named after a ham sandwich was reaching behind him for the usual oversized cheque for the $5,000 spending money part of the prize. It was then that she realised that she had won first prize and her mouth went dry. She should have been paying more attention rather than reminiscing about her family life. Then another even more terrifying thought hit her; what if she was expected to remember what she had dictated to Leisa that night. Oh help, if only she could remember. She nibbled her bottom lip in anxiety.

Fortunately she didn't have to remember because the arrogant 'ham sandwich' seemed in a hurry to get the proceedings over and move on. Probably an alcohol soaked party with a group of starlets and adoring fans. She was completely surprised when he slid his hand under her arm and steered her towards the chairs at the side murmuring that he wanted to 'get her up to speed' on the details of the prize.

'Are you sure this can't wait?' muttered Chelsea as she sat unceremoniously on the cold metal chair that the man indicated.

Jack's throat went dry. This was proving harder than he anticipated. Chelsea was obviously one woman who was hard to impress. He hadn't needed to see her at all but he wasn't going to miss this chance. He was a lawyer for God's sake; he could think on his feet, he would come up with something to say. Talk about the fine print, his muddled brain suggested.

'We should talk about the fine print,' he said bestowing his best smile on Chelsea, thinking as the words came out of his mouth that he was a prize idiot.

'At three in the morning!' exclaimed Chelsea.

Oh hell, introduce yourself, you idiot Jack. He put out his hand and said, 'I am Jack Devon, Miss Prentiss.'

'So you're not named after a ham sandwich then, you're named after a car hoist.'

Jack cleared his throat and when it came out as an impatient sound his heart sank. He was floundering. He was losing his touch. He could just imagine what his sisters would have to say. He had never been short of words before. But then he had never responded so instantly to a woman before. He doubted that he had even met someone like this woman.

His mind froze as she gazed up at him with huge clear questioning eyes. Her shoe was flying back and forth as she swung her foot restlessly.

Chelsea quelled her impatience. Honestly, what was wrong with the man? He was obviously a lawyer but he seemed to lack the basic clues of human interaction. Her eyes held his and he loosened his tie as he folded himself into the chair at her side.

'God, you're like human origami, aren't you,' trilled Chelsea as she observed the loose limbed way he had relaxed into the chair. Jack felt anything but relaxed under the cool assessing eyes of a woman who was impervious to his charm. He cleared his throat again, 'Look Miss ...'

'Prentiss,' prompted Chelsea, infuriatingly calm.

Now Jack was seriously ruffled, in the space of an hour he had been called a ham sandwich, a car hoist and now she was likening him to some ancient Japanese craft. After having beautiful women purr his name in the thralls of passion, this attitude was quite a shock.

'You could always quit while you're behind,' Chelsea suggested helpfully.

'Don't you mean 'ahead'?' he corrected.

'Not in your case darling, not in your case.' Chelsea pressed her advantage by removing her shoe and inspecting the blister on her heel. Blasted maddening woman, thought Jack, as he whistled his next words back through his teeth.

'Perhaps we can do this tomorrow,' he acquiesced as he began to fold his papers into the briefcase at his feet.

'That would be better, I'm sorry, but my best friend is in labour as we speak and she wanted, no *demanded*, that I stay until the announcement. However, by now she will have twisted her husband's arm off his body and probably taken siege of the entire drug cupboard so I really would appreciate it if we could do this...whatever it is, later. Here's a business card with my mobile number. Tomorrow then, but I maybe held up at the hospital with my new godchild so perhaps we can do this over the phone,' she suggested hopefully. 'It can't be that complicated, surely. She paused, 'Oh, that's right, you're a lawyer, I guess it can.'

Jack's mouth fell open, he couldn't help it. The vixen was patronising him. Not only did this woman refuse to use his name she seemed totally unimpressed by his status. She was completely nonchalant about the whole celebrity factor and the prize. She hadn't asked one question about the money, the holiday or the television show. Most people would kill for their fifteen minutes of fame. But Chelsea obviously wasn't 'most people'. He had expected squeals and excited hugs. Chelsea was grateful but casual. Perhaps he had been hoping she would wrap herself around him. He certainly had been completely unprepared for her reaction; not just to the prize but to him.

He was stunned but not defeated; he would regroup tomorrow. Smiling and willing himself to convey his utter compliance with this feisty slip of a woman he again reached out to shake her hand. Chelsea allowed this with a winning smile of her own and tilted her head to the side. Devastatingly attractive, she thought. Jack was encouraged until he thought he heard her mutter under her breath, 'Pompous prat' as she walked off now barefoot and limping down the Quay.

He watched her walk away trying to balance the clipboard as she stuffed her high heels into the back pockets of the tiny white overalls while the shoulder strap slipped off her shoulder revealing a bare expanse of glowing tan skin. She was wearing a purple boob tube under that sexy gear he noticed as his pulse quickened again. He was determined to do whatever it took to see her again. But next time he would call the shots. He needed a plan.

Chapter 3

'There's good news and bad news,' Leisa said. Chelsea groaned. She knew where this was going. Her best friend had a habit of confusing the two. The good news could really be bad, and the bad news could actually be good; or sometimes even worse. 'Go on then, put me out of my misery', muttered Chelsea, feeling rebellious. They had played this game of good news/bad news since they were children hiding from Chelsea's siblings under her mother's table and Leisa always enjoyed it more than Chelsea. Leisa usually strung out the game with so many additions and caveats that it became an epic.

'Obviously my godson is the good news,' Chelsea prompted cheerfully hoping to steer the conversation to a speedy optimistic end. 'Although he was supposed to be a girl, I was all ready to submerse myself in the whole pink experience.'

'You're changing the subject, as usual,' said Leisa folding her arms with her superior look of 'I'm not going to tell you if you don't behave' that was so familiar to their friendship.

'Oh, go on then control freak.' Chelsea was grinning broadly. It was so good to see Leisa looking so great when she had given birth just six hours ago at 4.00 am. Chelsea had arrived at Hornsby Hospital on the Maternity Ward just minutes after the delivery and was thrilled to meet her godson, Hayden Michael Randall. She'd been surprised and gratified to learn that Leisa had been through a dream labour and had neither twisted Mike's arm off nor had she laid siege to the drug cupboard.

Chelsea had been home to her apartment in Chatswood and had drifted into a dreamless deep sleep and had just arrived back at the hospital. Leisa and Mike had been too excited to sleep and Mike had just gone downstairs to the kiosk. After the agonizing wait of her pregnancy and the numerous hospital visits it was a relief indeed for the baby to arrive so swiftly and for Leisa to have come through so well. They had been prepared for all kinds of disaster but the universe had smiled on this family and no-one deserved it more than Leisa and Mike.

'The good news is that I had an easy labour and quick delivery, yay!' boasted Leisa punching the air.

'You already said that,' moaned Chelsea in exasperation. Really at this rate this would take forever.

'Get used to it, you're going to hear it a lot,' chirped Leisa. 'The bad news is that Mike has had a contract delayed and has very little work for January.' There was more coming, Chelsea knew it, there always was.

'Which means, that the good news is,' Leisa paused for effect making Chelsea moan again, 'Mike will be on hand for nappy duty and general housewifely chores. And the bad news is...'

'That he is really crap at it,' Chelsea offered.

'Well, there is that,' conceded Leisa, 'But don't interrupt. Where was I?'

'Mike the crappy housewife,' Chelsea prompted, not wishing to prolong the agony.

'Oh, yes,' continued Leisa, 'the bad news is that you don't have to move into my house and become my nursemaid and Hayden Michael's nanny for the next few weeks.'

'That's the bad news!' laughed Chelsea, 'You can do better than that.'

'And the good news is,' Leisa went on, warming to the game, 'you can take your prize holiday as soon as you like.' Chelsea had told Leisa about her win in the small hours of the morning but they hadn't said much about it as the arrival of the 'most beautiful baby in the world' had taken precedence over everything else.

'That reminds me,' muttered Chelsea, beginning to panic, 'What on earth did I tell you to write? I can't remember?'

'Honestly, Chelsea,' said Leisa chuckling, 'you are so pedantic about your writing, I am shocked that you didn't keep a copy and file it in triplicate like you do everything else. Or have a copy in some fireproof safe somewhere the way you writers do. It is in my office filed under H for Holiday Competition. You're not the only one with a system.' Leisa loved to tease Chelsea about her obsession to tidiness with her writing that didn't transfer to any other area, especially housework.

Mike appeared at the doorway to the room and two heads turned to greet him with exuberant smiles. He was carrying the biggest bunch of snapdragons that Chelsea had ever seen. They were Leisa's favourites; she called them 'talking' flowers.

'You want the good news or the bad news?' he began.

'Don't *you* start!' chimed both women.

'You've been at it already, haven't you?' Mike grinned. He had been entertained many times by the good news/bad news game and sometimes joined in himself but both of them had told him that he spoiled the whole thing with his masculine logic and 'get to the point' impatience. He bent and kissed his wife's head, calling her a clever thing and showed them both the photos of his new son on his mobile phone. There was much oohing and aahing until a nurse came to check on Leisa's blood pressure and other observations, telling them that she would bring the baby in after his first bath in 20 minutes. Mike gave Leisa the phone and she and Chelsea flicked back and forth admiring the baby photos.

Chelsea let out a shriek when she flicked onto earlier photos and saw some of the shots that had been taken the previous night at the Harbour for the calendar.

'Good grief,' shrieked Chelsea, 'You got these already?' But before Mike could answer she squealed again in surprise as she saw herself, well, not much of herself, just her legs in the air by the bed and her hand reaching up for the red rose that was flying through space.

'Oh yeah,' said Mike, 'That's the bad news, or maybe the good news, I never know which with you girls.'

'Oh dear,' moaned Chelsea, then instantly cheered up, 'At least you can't tell who it is, that's got to be a blessing.' She pulled a hopeful face.

'With those fabulous pins, who cares! Ouch,' said Mike as he deflected the slap that Leisa aimed at him. 'They might use that shot, the fondue looks great.' It was Chelsea's turn to pretend to slap him now. 'Geez, you women are violent! A man could get seriously hurt around you two. Brad sent the images by SMS, he said you were hysterical Chelsea.'

'Oh, that reminds me,' continued Mike, 'the good news is, you were on Telly last night Chels.' The Channel 7 News crew was there taking in the local flavour. They taped your routine and it was on the New Year's special broadcast.' Mike grinned, pleased with himself.

'Oh no! *Please tell me you're kidding*!' begged Chelsea, 'That's the bad news, not the good news!'

'I give up,' said Mike.

Chelsea sat in the car fingering the key to Leisa and Mike's house. She felt a sense of exhilaration. She was too hyped up to go back to her place and Leisa had given her a list of things she needed. Obviously Leisa had been expecting a Caesarean Section. Her doctor had warned them that she might need one because of her pre-eclampsia. Leisa hadn't packed anything apart from clothes obviously expecting to be a post-operative patient, right under the weather, and now she wanted magazines and books. Chelsea was quite familiar with Leisa's office as she had often filled in for one of the women that Leisa employed in her catering business.

She laughed again as she remembered Leisa's reaction to her description of the devastatingly handsome man she had dubbed the ham sandwich, 'You're the one always being called a ham Chelsea, watch out you don't get caught in the sandwich,' Leisa had warned. Chelsea had snorted and told Leisa that as delectable as this man was, he was a stuffed-shirt pasty-faced lawyer who had bored her to tears.

'Delectable huh?' mused Leisa with a knowing look.

'That was a purely artistic assessment,' said Chelsea with a mutinous air.

The pasty-faced lawyer in question had just gotten off the phone to his older sister Jade, who was responsible for the 'Daydream Island' competition and prize arrangements. Jack had been seconded to help with the promotion and the competition as a favour to her when she had been unable to attend because her son Jamie had needed emergency surgery the morning before just as she was due to catch her flight from Surfer's Paradise to Sydney. She worked for a PR and events management firm in Surfer's.

Jack had been dreading the job; he hated the constant social whirl that his three sisters thrived on. They were so like their mother, 'social butterflies' his father James Devon, had called them. He must be more like his father who had left his sophisticated wife and his lively family to live in Stanthorpe near the border between NSW and Queensland. His father had married a country vet. Jack did not want to think about any resemblance he had to his father. His father had hated the high powered law firm where he was partner in Surfer's and had opened a small private law practice in Stanthorpe, a few hours' drive from his former home and business. Now he was content with conveyance, surveying and home contracts.

'I thought men were supposed to trade up, not down,' Sylvia, Jack's mother had remarked bitterly after the divorce, 'But no, my husband has to leave me for a woman who is not only older than me but she is a frumpy animal doctor to boot.'

Jack had been 21 at the time and at the end of his law degree at Macquarie University in Sydney. He had been devastated at the separation of his parents. He had assumed he would practice law by his father's side and felt the loss of his father keenly especially as his father seemed quite content to remain in the country. Jack didn't return to Surfer's Paradise after he finished law but instead stayed on with Danson & Crichton where he worked his way up the firm. At 34 he now managed the corporate contract section dealing mainly with advertising agencies.

His father's visits to Sydney were sporadic and slightly stilted affairs and Jack had been loath to visit his father and second wife in their new life at Stanthorpe. The relationship had stalemated with neither expressing their views or feelings. Each was waiting for the other to make the first move. The situation had been compounded with the death of his mother two years ago after a protracted battle with breast cancer. He had already been living in Sydney for nearly ten years by the time his mother had died.

Even then he had been unable to breach the distance with his father. Since his mother's death his family life revolved around his three sisters in his regular holiday visits to Surfer's Paradise. His sisters were vocal enough for a small army. They filled any room and with two older than him, Jade and Emily, and one younger, Kylie, he had never lacked for affection. Or torture, he mused. He smiled as he remembered the lengths of the bribing Jade had resorted to yesterday in order to get him to present the competition prize.

'Who else am I going to get on the last day of the year? Everyone has left our office, and every office in Australia apparently. Please Jack, you can have our beach house for as long as you like, whenever you like, say you'll do it for your big sister who kept you out of trouble for all of your young useless life.'

'Alright Jade, don't overdo it. I will do it, but the fridge better be full of food and beer when I come to the beach house.'

'Of course, darling, love you, ciao.'

'Give my love to Jamie,' Jack said just before the phone clicked.

Jamie's surgery wasn't the only disaster he had to contend with, Jack mused. Just as well he was a meticulous planner. Not that it was his problem that there had been a fire in the hotel that was the competition prize venue. He had been very adamant that presenting the cheque was all he was prepared to do.

It had taken Jade off guard when he had volunteered to sort the other problems for her but because of her worry for her son she hadn't given him the usual sisterly inquisition, assuming he felt sorry for her situation. Jack fully intended to keep her in the dark about his interest in Chelsea. That shouldn't be difficult to achieve given her current level of distraction. His normally unflappable sister had been sick with worry for her son.

Jade had also been panicking because the television company that owned 'Daydream Island' was considering axing the show. This was always on the cards with any television show. Job insecurity went with the territory but it hadn't made her job easier

27

when the actors she had to deal with were suddenly disinterested in the promotion of the show, instead looking for other opportunities. Most had been relieved to have their commitments to the competition and the prize downscaled. No-one wanted a star struck fan living with them when they were under a cloud. Morale on set was at an all-time low.

The winner was supposed to be prepared to leave within four hours of winning the prize in a frantic airport dash that would be filmed. The competition had been advertised to appeal to fans who were seeking their fifteen minutes of fame and celebrity. The film crew from the soap opera had been organised to film the winner for the entire week as they travelled with them to Surfer's and lived in the same hotel as some of the actors. It was considered good advertising and would hopefully boost the flagging ratings.

The fire had changed all that. Fearing a publicity nightmare and expensive law suit the company had requested Jack to present a new prize package and it had been faxed by a grateful Jade to his city office just hours ago. The winner still had a walk-on role in the show and they would hang out with the actors but the accommodation and reality show aspect of the prize had been scrapped. He was to placate the winner about the changes. An entirely unnecessary gesture because Miss Chelsea Prentiss didn't know or care about the details of her prize. The organisers had expected a fame crazed winner and Chelsea was anything but that.

If Jade had wrongly assumed that he had cleverly cleared that hurdle with marvellous tactics and clever words he hadn't disabused her of the idea, he just smiled subtly. The truth was just the opposite. He hadn't got a word in and the situation had resolved itself. At least the first part. Now he had to tell Chelsea that she wouldn't be staying at the original venue with the cast and would only be filmed on set for a few hours. He didn't know how she would take that but if her casual attitude so far was anything to go by he didn't think he had much to worry about.

Jack Devon had his own agenda with Chelsea Prentiss. This feisty woman had piqued his interest as no other woman had. She was like a whirlwind rollercoaster and he decided that he was going along for the ride. After all, a week in paradise should give him the chance to show his best side and change her initial impressions. His office was closed for another 10 days; he could do with a holiday. He would accompany her to Surfer's Paradise. He closed his laptop with a satisfied snap. It was the first impulsive act in Jack Devon's carefully orchestrated life.

Now that he had taken care of the details he only had to convince Chelsea to meet him in person rather than engage in a hasty phone conversation. He had a plan for that as well, he thought smugly as he looked over the papers he had quickly drawn up for Chelsea to sign agreeing to the changes.

This time he was ready for her. He would get in first. A hastily arranged table in the Centrepoint Tower revolving restaurant, 360 named for its 360 degree views of the city, should be sufficient attraction. He hoped she was free for dinner, it was a gamble he was prepared to take.

He couldn't wait to see her again. He dialled her number.

Chapter 4.

In the end it had been too easy. Chelsea had agreed quite readily to meet him for dinner later that evening. Jack felt the purr of his Mercedes sports car as he wheeled into the scant evening traffic into the city and headed towards the Martin Place car park.

Chelsea was surprised at herself. She told herself that she had always wanted to dine at the Centrepoint Tower and eat in the revolving restaurant 360 Bar and Dining Restaurant. The food was reputed to be Sydney's finest. She certainly wasn't going to enjoy the view at close quarters, she had a morbid fear of heights but she was starving and it would be awhile before she would enjoy Leisa's cooking again. It was better than the salad wrap at the corner deli she had been planning when Jack had phoned.

She had been sitting in her car in the hospital car park. She had nearly jumped out of her skin and was a bit disorientated because she had just been thinking about him. She had been going over the shocking news delivered by an amused Leisa that she had been supposed to fly out immediately according to the prize conditions. 'Bother! I suppose had better meet with 'the stuffed shirt' then,' she'd said begrudgingly.

When she arrived at the restaurant at 5.00 pm Jack was already sitting in the lounge chairs that dotted the bar near the lifts. He had his laptop on the mahogany table in front of him. She was not to know this was merely a carefully orchestrated prop. 'Workaholic,' she muttered under her breath.

Seeing him was a shock. He had actually improved on last night. She realised that her assessment of him as pasty faced had been a mistake of the lighting. He had a healthy bronze glow. As he saw her he shut down his computer and gave her one of his devastating smiles. Chelsea knees gave a small wobble. She told herself that it was a simple reaction to the height of the building. Blasted phobia of heights.

Jack drew in a jagged breath; she looked sophisticated and beautiful. For the first time she seemed tentative, nervous. She was wearing a ballet length black dress that was strapless and had a soft lustre. She had a chiffon shawl that was a luminous black and it was pinned on one shoulder with an ebony clip. Her hair was piled up loosely on top of her head.

She had been quite dismayed last night when he had told her that there were some unavoidable changes to the arrangements for claiming the prize. Jack had reassured her that everything possible was being done to ensure her enjoyment and comfort and he would personally handle any problems.

She had thought him haughty. She had been correct in her assumption that he was a lawyer. Little did she know that Jack had spent the morning studying the prize conditions. He had also read the press releases about the show to get up to speed about the soap opera.

Chelsea had no idea that Jack's only connection to the

television show was a casual arrangement with his sister where he had merely replaced her to present the prize.

Chelsea sincerely hoped that the changes didn't require any more time spent on set. It would be her only foray into screen writing she thought. She was already dreading it but she would have to hold up her end of the bargain. If that meant making a fool of herself on television then so be it. It couldn't be any worse than the segment that had aired last night when she had hammed it up for the Arabian Nights scene. Mike had obligingly taped it and she had watched it when she picked up her winning piece on the way to the restaurant.

'So, no bruises from last night then?' she probed with a saucy smile as he joined her at the bar, referring to his collapsing chair accident.

'My fall wasn't nearly as entertaining as yours,' he countered, 'or as publicised.'

'Touché,' Chelsea gurgled showing even white teeth, 'I didn't know the news crew was there until my best friend's husband told me later.'

'I suspected as much,' Jack said, disarmed by her naturalness and lack of pretence.

'At least you didn't see yourself,' she said, 'you were spared that nightmare.'

'It didn't look like a nightmare from where I was sitting. I enjoyed the view.'

What a charming devil he was now that he was relaxed. He gallantly put a hand under her arm to lead her to a table when he felt her freeze. Jack noticed the imperceptible reaction and wondered what had caused it with a worrying frown.

Chelsea hesitated. All the air had left her lungs and she was overcome with nausea. She gripped the side of the nearest chair in fear. For the first time she had seen the full 360 degree view. The glass windows that encompassed the restaurant were floor to ceiling and the tower had seemed to move. Breathe, breathe; she willed herself. She saw with relief the table Jack was moving towards was not near the view and she sunk gratefully into the chair he held for her.

The waiter came to take their order and Jack was gracious, allowing her to order. Jeff had been threatened by a woman who made her own choices and she enjoyed Jack's security in his manhood. She ordered the deep-fried crumbed mushroom and baby cos salad. Jack ordered Tournedos of Black Angus Beef and asked her which wine she preferred. 'I'm no wine buff, you do the honours.' At least he wasn't trying to show off. So many of her friends had longer discussions over wine lists than they did over political elections.

Chelsea wondered if he was married. He wasn't wearing a ring, but that didn't always mean anything. There was no tan line either. What was she thinking? She gave herself a mental shake.

'So do you come here often?' he queried gently, desperate to know more about her.

'Never been', she said, avoiding the teasing quality in his voice.

'I'm surprised, a city girl who hasn't seen the sights.'

That has the desired effect of her opening up to him about her life. 'I don't know if I am really a city girl. I loved the country as a child but we moved so around so much I never got the chance to belong anywhere.'

The conversation flowed easily after that. She told him of her job at the preschool and her freelance writing. Her intelligent eyes were utterly beguiling and her razor sharp wit had him laughing freely. He could have sat there forever watching her face light up and her expressive hands waving as she recounted her experiences at the preschool and talked about her gypsy childhood. She was a born storyteller. The short piece she'd written for the competition didn't begin to show her talent. He suspected that she had greater depth than most people knew.

Chelsea couldn't believe that she was so comfortable in Jack's presence. He rested his face on his hand, his long elegant fingers framing his mouth. A mouth that smiled so readily, so spontaneously; a smile that reached to those marvellous sparkling eyes. He was so much more interesting than she had given him credit for. Even though she had talked a great deal he had been more than able to converse and to her surprise he had an irreverent sense of humour that she found fascinating as he told her about his clients.

She realised that even though they had been chatting for ages she still didn't know where he lived and suddenly found herself wondering if she would see him in Surfer's Paradise. She tried to think of a way to find out but couldn't think of a casual question that would sound as bland as she wished.

Before long they had finished their meals and Chelsea realised with a shock that they had been talking for two hours and she hadn't been bored for a moment. Jack had only filled her glass once and she had enjoyed the subtle earthy flavour of the red wine.

She was so relaxed she had forgotten to ask about the prize. The waiter brought the desert trolley that was an extravagant affair. 360's Bar and Dining was world renowned for its desert menu. Chelsea decided on the sample plate that was a specialty of the restaurant.

When they had finished Jack inquired, 'Would you like to see the view?'

'Oh God no, I hate heights! I am just fine over here, thanks. It is hard enough to deal with the slight swaying of the place.' So that was it, he thought, she'd been reacting to the height and not him.

'I'm sorry we could have gone somewhere else. You should have said.'

'Don't get me wrong, I have been dying to come to this place; and it has lived up to the hype. I just don't want to get any closer to those huge glass windows. I might be forced to remember that I am precariously placed in a restaurant on a tower that is higher than I have ever been that looks like a matchstick from the distance. I am terrified of the prospect of staying in a high rise hotel at Surfer's; I hear they have over 40 storeys. Please tell me I don't have to go to sleep at night worrying that I have 6,000 people above me and the ground miles below me. Which hotel am I staying at?'

Jack made a lightning decision. 'No, there is a really modern beach house where you can relax and unwind.'

Jade might kill him but he could cancel the hotel suite that was designated for Chelsea and she could stay at Jade's beach house. He knew it was empty because their sister Kylie had gone overseas instead of her planned stay in the beach house. The television studio would be glad to recoup the cost of the hotel, especially with the hotel fire causing problems. Jade and Andrew had bought the house as an investment property. He had already organised to stay with Jade and Andrew in their luxury home on the famous Broadwater along the canals that was a scenic part of Surfer's Paradise.

Anyway, Jade owed him big time. At least that was how he would put it to her and if she questioned why he had chosen that time to come to Surfer's he would say he was helping her out of a hole and it was about time he came to visit his fabulous sister and her family.

'Thank God,' she breathed; her relief palpable. It was ample reward to Jack.

Twice tonight he had seen inside the woman and sensed her vulnerability. She seemed so fearless. He felt privileged to be granted a deeper view of this woman who made him feel so alive.

She was beginning to look a little guarded. He didn't want to spook her. It was time to deal with the details. He reluctantly slipped into professional mode and took his papers out of his briefcase. She saw a copy of the competition entry and her fingers itched to take it. She hadn't been able to find Leisa's copy in her office files and she wasn't about to bother her best friend while she was in hospital.

'Do you happen to have another copy of that? I seem to have misplaced mine,' she tried to say it as blandly as she could but by the responding twinkle in his eye she knew she had been found out.

'You don't have any idea what you wrote do you?'

'No, don't remember. I know it was a cheeky send up and somebody set fire to a newspaper.'

He held it tauntingly just out of reach. He was playing with her. She gave him a dark threatening look.

'I guess I could let you have it for a quick minute to refresh your memory.'

She reached. He withdrew.

'You wretched man!'

'It would be really embarrassing for you to arrive there with no memory of your own ideas,' he taunted. He was loving this.

'I'll claim amnesia; every soap opera has to have a little amnesia, its obligatory.'

'But you have to help with the scene.' He stretched back in his seat, this was better, now he had managed to turn the tables on her.

'You're kidding!. Now he was chuckling and wiping his eyes. This was getting better by the minute.

'You sound suspiciously like a woman who hasn't even read the competition details.'

'I haven't.'

Now he threw his head back and roared laughing. Her lack of pretence was adorable.

His laugh rumbled through her and touched a part of her that had been asleep for a very long time, perhaps forever. She had never had a man who got such a kick out of listening to her. Those intelligent laughing eyes were sexier than any thighs she had ever seen. She liked this playful side of him.

Chelsea had no choice but to relate the whole sorry tale. About dictating some nonsense to Leisa while she was trying to follow Leisa's cooking instructions with Mike helping who had ten thumbs.

'What makes a woman decide to cook six chocolate soufflés with Laurel and Hardy in the kitchen is beyond me! We should have stuck to crepes; at least they can't get any flatter.'

Jack was enchanted.

'Do I really have to act in the scene I wrote? Give me a look you beast!'

'How are you naked under a beach robe?'

Chelsea pounced, snatching the paper. Jack sat back and watched the changing emotions on her face as they passed like a rapid movie screen across her expressive face as she read.

Blair was late again. He did this deliberately; Brittany just knew. It was bad enough that he spent weeks on the road with that grungy rock band 'Splinters'. But then to come home and walk straight back out again to spend ages at the gym when he knew she wanted to see him, ached to be with. It was too much.

She heard his key in the door. She resolved that she wouldn't be a bitch. She was sorry about last Friday night. He had been away for a week and then only seemed interested in the sports coverage. When he had reached to hold her, beer in hand, while still watching some woman parading around in a bikini on television, with pert breasts thrust out, she had snapped.

She had gone to sleep in the spare room and made sure their electric blanket had been on high on both sides so that when he went to bed in the cloying summer heat he would as annoyed as she was. When he had asked her in the morning, 'What was that all about?' she had sniped, 'You wanted your bed hot; I gave it to you hot!.

But she truly hadn't meant to cook his tomato and eggs with disinfectant instead of oil, she simply hadn't seen in the candlelight that she had set up for a cosy night in. That ruined the seduction that night. But tonight everything would go smoothly. She was naked under her beach robe.

She kissed him at the door, got him a beer from the fridge, and sat opposite him at the kitchen bench, perching sexily. She had just allowed the robe to 'accidentally' slip open when he reached—for the newspaper. She reached—for the cigarette lighter and calmly and thoughtfully set the newspaper on fire.

'Oh dear, this is worse than I remember. Is it too late to back out?'

'Absolutely.' He was being mean; and loving every entertaining minute of it. Her eyes grew huge and anguished.

'You're loving this aren't you?'

'Yes.'

'You have no pity.'

'No.'

'You have no soul.'

'No, I'm a lawyer. We have our souls surgically removed in our first year at University.'

'I could believe that.'

'Sad but true.'

He took pity on her. 'No, you don't have to do *that* scene, of course, it was written for the main characters.' When he saw the surprise in her eyes he said, 'Oh my God, you don't even know the characters, do you?'

When she gave an imperceptible shake of her head he said, 'Have you ever actually watched the show, by any chance?'

'Well, it was on one night when I was over at Leisa's painting her toe nails. She couldn't reach them anymore because she was too huge to bend over. Being pregnant, you know. But I don't remember much. Leisa filled me in on two of them and said the wife was being ignored and I took it from there. I had no idea they were the lead characters.' Chelsea's voice became thinner.

'Well, I can see I will have to take you in hand.'

'Oh really?' She liked the way he said that; there was a hidden promise in his dark eyes.

'Yes really. I think it is high time you had some private tuition on this very poorly researched subject. Shame on you.'

Jack didn't know a thing about the show, but by the time he had Leisa sitting down to watch past episodes to get a handle on the show he would be an expert. His sisters would help. He would be bankrupt with all the bribes he had planned for just the next week. It would be worth it.

'And you're the man to do it, I suppose?'

'I'm the man to do it.'

Chapter 5

It had been a huge relief to Chelsea when she found out that she had avoided having to fly out immediate after receiving the prize. It might make good television to film a frantic dash to the airport in the early hours of the morning but Chelsea shuddered at the thought. She really should have paid more attention to Leisa. She didn't remember anything about the prize conditions but Leisa had probably told her when she was filling in the forms for Chelsea and she had done what her mother always accused her of, filing it in her head under 'miscellaneous'.

She was very grateful to Jack for smoothing that problem over although she didn't want to feel indebted to him. She had always been uncomfortable relying on any man. She was relieved when she had been able to leave the morning after her dinner with Jack. He had handed presented her ticket at the end of their evening and had said casually that he would be flying with her. She had been able to pack and get ready for their 5.00 am flight and say a quick late-night good-bye to Leisa as well.

She looked at Jack's lean body as he slept in the plane next to her. There wasn't really much room for his long legs but these had been the only seats available at short notice and even though she had only had a few hours' sleep Chelsea was too excited to rest. She told herself that had nothing to do with the tall man at her side.

Jack tensed. It was hard to pretend to be sleeping but if he looked in Chelsea's rapt face and was so close to those kissable lips he wouldn't be able to control himself for long. Better for him to pretend to sleep.

Chelsea smiled as she remembered her late night visit to Leisa. Leisa had given her blessing. She had insisted that Chelsea listen to her horoscope and not the lecture that Chelsea had been expecting.

'Listen to this Chels. 'A windfall has come your way and it is time to seize new opportunities. Get on that plane. New locales await those brave enough to use their wings and fly. Jupiter is rising and January is a golden opportunity. Long awaited resolutions are around the corner'.'

'*Here! You made that up!*' shrieked Chelsea, snatching the magazine.

'I did not, what kind of a best friend do you take me for?' said Leisa. 'Well it *is* a golden opportunity. It isn't as if you had anything else planned Chels; the preschool is closed until the 16th.'

Chelsea settled back into the seat and tried to relax. It was no good. She was far too excited to rest. She was disappointed that Jack had fallen asleep. She had been surprised at how much she had enjoyed his company.

The man certainly wasn't dull. She smiled as she thought of the story he had told her about one of his elderly clients who had been taken in by a swindler. It was the usual story of a conman posing as a tradesman. The conman had promised to paint her house and had mistakenly thought that Geraldine, the old dear, was more incapacitated than she was, he certainly must have thought her stupid. He had brought ladders and equipment. When Geraldine had gone outside to take him a glass of homemade lemonade not long after he had started she was shocked to find that he was not painting but splashing water around.

Geraldine had quietly and coldly put the glass of lemonade on the wrought iron table at the back of the house and had gone to the garden shed and taken one of her own cans of paint and promptly thrown it over the unsuspecting conman, telling him that he obviously didn't 'know paint from water and God help him if he ever showed his face again.' She recalled the way Jack's face lit up with amusement as he told her the story. He was a great storyteller and had waved his hands and imitated Geraldine perfectly. She had experienced a flash of familiarity; his sense of humour was so like her own.

Chelsea shook that thought away. She didn't want to sit here next to this virile man and think about what they had in common. Careful not to disturb Jack she slipped her laptop out of the animal print briefcase at her feet. If she was going to have to endure this dreadful television prize experience she might as well write about the whole thing. It wasn't long before she was typing furiously and had all but forgotten the handsome man at her side.

The handsome man in question was having a much harder time. It had seemed a good idea to pretend to nod off but now he was cramped and uncomfortable. He was having a great deal of trouble keeping his thoughts from wandering to Chelsea. She was engrossed in her writing and didn't seem to notice that her arm was occasionally bumping his. This was not helping him keep his mind off her.

He slowly adjusted his position so that he could see the screen of her computer. He might as well get some entertainment out of the situation. It had been a hasty decision to accompany Chelsea but he had managed to sound as if this was planned all along and part of the package. He had been pleased with himself for the way he handled things. As long as his garrulous sister didn't put her foot in it and rattle on in front of Chelsea things would be fine.

He moaned. In a pig's eye would his sister miss a chance to embarrass him. If he did ask her to co-operate there would be the inevitable teasing that she felt was her birthright. He would avoid her; that should work. He smiled to himself until he realised that Jade was bound to be right in the middle of everything as the consultant for the public relations firm representing the television studio.

With his headrest lowered he observed Chelsea and read her words without her seeing him. He was soon engrossed in the tale she was telling. Why the little vixen was relating the story of Geraldine and the painter, titled, 'Karma of a Different Hue'. Damn she was good. He suppressed a chuckle as he read the rollicking version with the additions of Chelsea's imagination. There was now a psychic marmalade cat that Geraldine consulted with regard to everything, 'feline painting advice'.

He chuckled and Chelsea's concentration was lost as she looked straight into his dark humour-filled eyes. They really were the most incredible chocolate brown.

'You're very good,' he murmured.

'Why thank you,' Chelsea said, for once a little flustered.

'A lot of lawyers become writers you know. Their job serves as years of research into the criminal mind. And you must deal with fiction on a daily basis: surely?' she added.

'I am afraid there is not much drama in corporate contracts. All clauses and amendments. Boring stuff.'

'But you sound like you love it.'

'I do. I chose it because I had so much experience with dad in his firm. I guess I always assumed that I would just join him after I graduated. Being in the office was the only time I got to really hang out with him.'

'And now?'

Jack's eyes clouded. 'I have seen very little of him in the last decade. When he left us and divorced mum to marry his mistress I just assumed that he wanted out of our lives. The only time I see him is when he has to come to Sydney on business or when he is visiting back in Surfer's.'

'I mean about the law, are you still happy with the choice? Were you doing it for your dad or yourself?' The question disconcerted him. He had never considered the ins and outs of that decision. It had seemed like a natural choice.

'You really turn over every rock don't you? I guess that's the writer in you.'

'And you answer every question with a question. I guess that's the lawyer in you.'

'Touché.'

She sensed his discomfort. 'You don't mind me stealing your story? You won't sue me will you? Perhaps Geraldine will, oh dear.'

He laughed a cracking laugh. 'She would absolutely love it, the old terror. She told me at the time that she wanted to go to the media but I advised her against it. With the poor sorry conman only a teenage boy and crying his eyes out, covered in paint, she did not look the victim, frail elderly be damned.' A thought struck him. 'You must meet her, I will introduce you to her, she would be thrilled.' His eyes were alight with humour.

'I would love that.'

He extended his hand towards the computer. 'May I?'

'Be my guest.' She was secretly thrilled at his interest as his long capable fingers manipulated the mouse and scrolled down the computer. He chuckled as he read. He had told her that he had enjoyed representing Geraldine when she had been sued by the family of the teenager who had conned her. It was a change from the corporate boardroom he had said. Geraldine was the grandmother of his associate and friend Scott.

Chelsea saw Jack's animation when he talked about Geraldine and she hoped that he would make good on his suggestion to introduce Chelsea to her. She sounded like Ezzie the woman who lived in their street when Leisa and Chelsea were children. She had incorporated the story of Ezzie into the story of Geraldine's adventure with the conman. She nervously chewed her lip as Jack read the story she had just written and incorporated into a previous story that was about her childhood.

Ezzie, aka Esmeralda, was known and loved for her spectacular parties for little girls whose mothers worked long hours in the nearby food production factory. While mothers wore hairnets at the factory the little girls wore every other kind of hat at Ezzie's place. Ezzie was an old lady, much older than their mothers. She held parties because she loved them; she invited little girls because she loved them too.

Ezzie never scolded about mess or noise. She served dainty food on elegant plates. Those parties were just for little girls. No adult parties where the children were banished outside. No, here at Ezzie's they were the guests of honour. No boys to annoy, not even brothers. Just little girls and Ezzie. Even their mothers just dropped them off in their summer dresses and came back later to get their excited daughters who were weary from games and full of cake.

Chelsea and Leisa had lived side by side back then, in the mists of childhood. Chelsea's grandmother Nana Greerson lived next to Leisa's family. The two girls had become instant and lifelong friends. Chelsea's parents had lived in half the old federation house with their four children and Nana had lived in the other half. Chelsea had hated leaving. She loved everything about that street and Tamworth.

Chelsea and Leisa had sat and talked under the table with the lace tablecloth draped to the floor hiding them. They lived in their own world, chubby little fingers colouring, playing, and words flowing effortlessly between friends. Leisa would sit one leg under her and the other sticking straight out 'to nowhere' as her mother said. Even then her soft fine hair hung 'straight as sticks' as her mother said, pushed back continually by pudgy fingers; bright expressive eyes leaping and catching at everything around her.

While Leisa chattered and sang Chelsea usually lay reading with one hand propping her chin up and the other hand holding the book that she was currently devouring. Chelsea would be curled up in any available corner and Leisa would be stretched out carelessly, with her legs sticking out from under the haven of the lace tablecloth. If they were caught hiding there by one of Chelsea's twin brothers Mitchell or Terry, Chelsea would berate Leisa for leaving her legs sticking out where the boys would see them and find them. For when their hiding place was discovered the peace of their world was over. Leisa was an only child and could never remember to hide properly much to Chelsea's disgust.

Chelsea had been delighted when she had returned to the home of her childhood to find Leisa still living next door. The two friends took up where they left off as if the intervening years had melted away. Ezzie, of course was long gone. Chelsea and all the little girls had missed the old woman they had grown to love. She missed the life the family had enjoyed in the big rambling house with the wide verandas of her grandmother. The family had struggled with near poverty conditions as the money from their father was erratic. It had been such a boon to them for Nan Greerson to leave her daughter the family home after her death. It had provided the family with the first real sense of security in years.

Jack read the story of Geraldine and Ezzie and the little girls and wondered how much of Chelsea's life was in the story of the two old irascible ladies who lived side by side and were lifelong friends.

He longed to see into Chelsea's world. He found the story enchanting. At the end of the story was a photo of two tiny girls. One had wispy blonde hair that was long and straight. The other had caramel curls. Both were in frothy party dresses. The blonde girl was standing straight to the camera, alert and poised and the other, who he assumed was Chelsea was looking away into the horizon; she was miles away. Probably inventing some story or other.

'This is you?' he asked, pointing at the tiny girl with the caramel hair.

'Yes, pretty easy to pick isn't it?' she said with a wry smile.

'You are miles away in this photo, were you making up some story? Imagining another place and time perhaps?'

'Nothing that interesting, I'm afraid,' she answered modestly, 'My balloon had drifted into the cow paddock and I was watching it and waiting until I the photo was finished so I could climb over the railing fence and chase it.'

Jack laughed a rippling laugh and returned the lap top to her brushing her arm with his as he did. Chelsea felt a shiver of delight run up her arm. I must be tired, she thought. What is wrong with me? I can't possibly find this man attractive. Can I?

'The story is enchanting, you're very good at what you do, Chelsea Prentiss.' His eyes held hers and the shiver she was trying to deny travelled through her body.

'You're too kind.'

'Have you been published?' He was curious about her.

'Just a few short stories in magazines. I did creative writing as my elective at Uni. It's just a hobby really.'

Jack admired her humility. She was really talented.

'Well, if it means anything that a grown man can enjoy the story of two little country girls and a pair of old ladies, then it should be more than a hobby.' Chelsea blushed; warmed by the expected praise.

Jack was a regular traveller and brought a travel checker board out of his briefcase much to Chelsea's delight.

'And here I was assuming you were a blatant workaholic,' said Chelsea.

'You know what they say about first impressions,' he said sagely. 'I challenge you to a checkers tournament. Best out of three.'

The flight to Coolangatta was just over an hour and the time passed so quickly that Chelsea felt they had only just taken off. On their arrival at the Gold Coast Airport Jack quickly picked up the hire care he had arranged. Chelsea was beginning to feel a little overwhelmed. It appeared that Jack was in command of all the arrangements and she wondered when she would meet the entourage of people that she was expecting from the television studio.

Jack seemed to sense her disquiet and kept up an interesting commentary. He told her that the Gold Coast Airport had an interesting history. The runway itself straddled the twin cities of Tweed Heads and Coolangatta and that these cities were each side of the Queensland and New South Wales borders. The only travel Chelsea had done was with the family following her father's endless quest for the perfect job and home. She felt a rising excitement. She was finally going to have a holiday on the beach, the dream of her childhood. She was relieved that Jack was taking a professional air with her and she began to relax and enjoy the trip.

On their arrival a tall slim woman threw her arms around Jack. Twirling her in the air, Jack planted a huge kiss on her cheek. He was grinning like a Cheshire cat. Chelsea felt an unexpected pang. Her mind wandered to wondering what it would be like to be on the receiving end of one of those kisses.

'Welcome to 'Paradise'. I'm Jade Corley. I hope my brother has taken good care of you.'

Chelsea warmed to her immediately. She was bright and chatty and quickly filled Chelsea in on the week's schedule while handing her a selection of tourist brochures.

Jade had been in a right state of anxiety with all the adjustments that she thought she had to make to the arrangements and had been immensely relieved when Jack told her that she could drop half of the media circus that was originally planned for the winner.

Jade had confided to Jack over the phone, 'the inside word is that the show will be axed. It could happen in days but we have to keep a lid on it.' When he had told her that Chelsea was quite happy with the changes she had responded with a meaningful sigh. 'Thank God our girl is easy-going; some fans would sue us six ways 'til Sunday.'

Chelsea gripped the side of the passenger seat of the car as Jade wove in and out of the holiday traffic speedily and chatted all the way. Her expressive hands were laden with bracelets and jingled as she gestured dramatically.

'She drives the way she talks,' explained Jack, earning a fierce look from his doting sister for his words.

'Just you wait brother dear, or I shall feel compelled to reveal all the secrets of your misguided youth,' Jade threatened.

'Chelsea isn't vaguely interested in family gossip about me. She thinks I'm dead boring,' said Jack, causing Chelsea to blush profusely.

'On the contrary,' she purred, 'I'm all ears!' She gave Jade an expressive wink. Jack groaned.

'This is the price I have to pay for taking loving care of a houseful of women,' he grumbled. 'Traitors all of them.'

Jade and Chelsea laughed.

'How do you feel about winning the prize, Chelsea? I saw the televised segment of the prize presentation. I must say you weren't the typical winner screaming and running around for joy,' said Jade.

'I am very excited to be here. I have always wanted a beach holiday,' she said diplomatically.

'You must be thrilled to be on 'Daydream Island'. Many of my friends said they'd kill for the chance,' Jade said.

'Oh, that,' Chelsea said flatly.

'She doesn't even watch the show,' said an amused Jack from the back seat.

'Dobber!' accused Chelsea, throwing Jack a black look.

Jade squealed with delight. 'I think I'm going to like you Chelsea Prentiss.'

'It's true I'm afraid. I'm a complete fraud as far as fans go,' Chelsea admitted.

Chapter 6

Gavin Blake was at the centre of yet another on-set drama. He was loudly protesting his complaints about the current scene when Chelsea arrived with Jade and Jack. As the star of 'Daydream Island' he was the resident prima donna.

Chelsea was quite taken aback to realise that he was openly gay when Jack had told her that Gavin played the penultimate playboy romancing woman after woman on the show. He was so convincing in the seduction scene that was being filmed. She was amazed when he switched on flawlessly for the camera, and then reverted to his natural self when the camera was off. But he was an actor, so Chelsea wondered what his 'natural self' could possibly be when so much of his life involved performance.

The cast was warm and welcoming and most of them were happy to take a break and talk to Chelsea. Gavin muttered 'You're welcome to the whole sorry mess—the day is a waste anyway.'

'So you're a perfectionist then?' Chelsea shot back at him

without a pause.

'Ah, understanding at last,' Gavin said, throwing his arm around Chelsea and commandeering her for a tour.

'Peasants the lot of them,' muttered Gavin as he steered Chelsea towards a hallway. 'I can't handle tantrums before lunch.'

'Unless you're the one throwing it?' laughed Chelsea gaily, as she allowed Gavin to lead her.

'The artistic temperament darling,' explained Gavin, 'it's a complete slave driver.'

'And you're milking it for all its worth.'

'Too true, too true,' agreed Gavin. 'Tell me, what job do you have in the civilian world that gives you such fantastic insights into human nature?'

'I work in a preschool,' Chelsea offered and was delighted when Gavin gave a roaring laugh and said, 'I'm really going to like you Chelsea Prentiss. You will need your preschool training with this lot, m'dear—me included.'

'Tell me,' he whispered, with a conspiratorial air. 'Who is the gorgeous hunk you came with? He has a body to die for.'

'That is Jack Devon. He's the company lawyer.'

'Oh really. That *is* interesting. I wonder what his presence means. There's been talk the show will be axed. I wonder if that's why he is here. Do you know anything, my sweet?'

'Haven't a clue,' said Chelsea truthfully. If only Gavin knew how little she did know. She would have to get the DVD's of the show from Jack and watch them tonight so that she could at least catch up with the current story line.

Gavin took her through to the salon and make up room where a voluptuous aboriginal girl was sorting through small glass pots, brushes and colourful nail polishes. The girl looked up when Chelsea and Gavin arrived and gave a mock sigh.

'What are you doing back here Gazza? Did you wipe off one of those million layers of foundation and find the real you yet?'

'This is Emma, magician extraordinaire, she takes us all from drab to fab, it is just a shame that she isn't mute, the sharp tongued harpy.' Gavin grinned broadly.

Emma threw a towelette at Gavin and he bowed theatrically.

'She really loves me, you know,' he crooned at Emma, '*This* is the real glamour end of the business.' He gestured eloquently with an arm to indicate the beauty salon with its rows of mirrors and lights. 'This is where the real secrets are laid bare.' He winked at Chelsea.

Emma made a scornful sound and rolled her eyes.

'It's true, you know,' he said, sitting backwards on one of the chrome chairs. He rifled through the make-up drawer in front of him. Emma swatted his hand. 'You're a pain Gazza, leave my stuff alone! Go back on set, they need you, I don't!'

'Catty, catty! I am finished for the day, I've been up since 4.00 am, I am fit to be tied and I am going home for some shut eye.' Gavin turned to Chelsea. 'Well, my sweet, I will leave you here in Emma's capable hands. I am obviously unwanted by *some* people,' he said, glaring pointedly at Emma but blowing her a kiss anyway.

'What do you mean leave me here?' Chelsea said with a rising sense of panic. She had never been a great fan of beauty treatments, her inability to sit still had her chafing at the hair salon for even the quickest hairstyling.

'Just a bit of pampering, my sweet,' said Gavin on his way out the door. Chelsea turned to Emma in alarm.

'Exactly what did you have in mind, Emma? I really don't have time...'

'We have to practice your make up, but we don't have to do that today. I will just do a little cleansing, put in a mask, manicure, pedicure, that sort of thing; they have given me two hours to work with you.' The sideways look she gave Chelsea and the tone of her voiced seemed to infer that it would take more than two hours to make Chelsea even remotely human.

Emma was not impressed with the wide eyed look of panic in Chelsea's eyes or the reluctant way she slumped into the chrome chair near the door. Honestly, the damn actors were fussy enough. She didn't need this little nobody giving her attitude. At least the actors couldn't get enough of her; and here she had Miss 'Ooh Leave Me Alone' Prize Winner who looked like she would rather throw herself under a bus than have Emma's well-paid sought-after attention. She was going to hate every minute of this.

Emma sighed and indicated that Chelsea sit in one of the two large peeling black vinyl chairs in the centre of the room. Chelsea made an attempt at a gracious smile while quietly grinding her teeth. She sat in the chair opposite Emma, placing her hands on a faded green towel that was resting on the narrow table between them following Emma's careless gestures. Oh help, she isn't even going to speak to me, thought Chelsea. I am going to hate every minute of this.

'You could do with false nails, these are dreadful, what *do* you do?' questioned Emma as she threw Chelsea a disparaging glance and pulled a container filled with clear plastic nails out of a narrow drawer. Chelsea blanched, good grief, those things were like claws.

'I'm a preschool teacher,' said Chelsea warily, feeling that this was equivalent to being a war criminal with the way Emma was eyeing her.

'Figures!' sniped Emma.

Apparently that was the end of the conversation. Emma worked quietly and efficiently; filing, snipping, gluing the false nails, then trimming and lacquering them. Chelsea was not often intimidated but she sat silently while Emma soaked her feet in a foot spa, wrapped a towel around her head and applied a dubious looking thick green mask to her face.

Emma put toe separators between Chelsea's toes in preparation to lacquer her nails. The phone shrilled in the adjoining room. Emma pulled a lever that elevated the chair and then flicked a switch on the armrest with impossibly long red nail and wordlessly left the room, apparently to answer the phone. Chelsea jumped as the chair under her came to life with a rattling murmur. It was a massage chair. Ooh, I love a good massage, thought Chelsea.

Chelsea could hear Emma chatting and laughing. So the shrew can laugh, she thought; who would have thought it? It sounded like Emma was settling into a long conversation. The seat began to pinch, the massage sections buzzed and made her skin itch, the mask was getting tighter, her legs were going numb. Just as the towel slipped over one eye she spied Jack coming down the corridor with his suit coat slung over his shoulder.

'Hey Stretch!' she yelled, 'In here, help!'

Jack walked through the door to find Chelsea with green gunk over her face, towel over one eye, some white thing holding her toes apart, and an expression of sheer desperation. She was sliding down the chair that was over a foot in the air and was waving to him with long bright red nails.

'Don't just stand there Stretch,' wailed Chelsea. 'Get me out of here!'

Not for the first time since meeting Chelsea, Jack stood in front of her open-mouthed. What the hell was she up to now? Was there no end to her disasters? And yet another name; he was Stretch now?

'You didn't tell me about the torture clause Stretch,' moaned Chelsea. 'Get me out of here, quick, while Lucretia Borgia is gone! She's a sadist.'

Jack continued to stare nonplussed. Chelsea realised he was suffering from some sort of shock and began to talk, slowly and calmly as if she was talking to a hyperactive child with sugar overload.

'Take those wretched things off my toes, I can't use these damn fingernails that sadist glued on me. Then, pull that lever at the side so I can be reunited with mother earth. I'm ready for blastoff up here. Houston we have a problem.'

'This blasted chair feels like a thousand potholes, I thought I was back in the bush. Wonder the thing didn't take off without me.' Chelsea stabbed at the controls to turn the massage dial off and looked up to see the lawyer who prided himself on his control laughing so riotously that he was wiping his eyes on his rolled up shirt sleeve.

'There is nothing remotely funny about this Stretch, if you don't stop that I will have to slap some sense into you. This is torture, you should inform Amnesty International. Beauty treatments be damned! This is sheer unadulterated mutilation of the human form. What next? Will they cover us in honey and put us on ant nests to combat wrinkles! Count me out!'

Jack found the lever and the chair hissed into life sinking to floor level again.

'Thank God,' Chelsea said, leaping out of the chair.

She kept the scalding chatter up as she threw water on her face and peeled circles of green gunk off her face. Jack was sure he had never heard or seen anything this hilarious in his life. He sunk onto the nearest chair and collapsed into uncontrolled laughter. He held his side where a muscle ached from the strain. He hadn't laughed this much in years. I'm in love, he thought.

'There is seriously something wrong with you, Stretch,' muttered Chelsea. She made another ineffective swipe at her face, then throwing on her shoes and grabbing her bag she caught a handful of Jack's shirt and dragged him through the door with her.

'Freedom at last,' she sighed as they sat in the staff tea room minutes later.

'What are you going to tell Emma?' queried Jack more out of

curiosity than actual concern.

'I will tell her that she was gone so long I raised three children and solved world peace. I will ask her where she got her Sadist License. I will ask her what I did to her to deserve such torture. You'd think I stole her first born.'

'Some people pay good money for what you just had.' chuckled Jack.

'Yes, and some people swim with sharks and jump out of planes,' muttered Chelsea mutinously.

Jack was still laughing. 'You can't imagine what you looked like; a furious cute little swamp creature.'

'I had that coming I guess,' she gurgled, 'after all the names I've given you.' God, the man was gorgeous when he laughed. So she was 'cute', she thought. A woman would be happy every day of her life to look into those melting brown eyes when they sparkled with life and humour.

She is utterly captivating, he thought; I want more of her.

'Jack said you were happy to spend time away from the set,' Jade said. The three of them were walking down the avenue that began in the city and ended at the beach. 'I'm so relieved. Things are crazy here at the moment. Not just on set. The fire department has closed the entire hotel down where you were originally going to stay. I'm afraid my son having surgery has complicated things. I would have been available to show you around, but I hope you are ok with Jack filling in for me.'

Jade had been more than happy to offer the beach house that she and her husband Andrew had bought two years ago. She was grateful to Jack for taking over the task of soothing the competition debacle. It had been a nightmare from start to finish. The television production company had been demanding and difficult and she would be glad when the current promotion was over.

'I'm really looking forward to seeing a few of the shops. I'm told the swimsuits are to die for.' Chelsea's eyes lit up.

'You have to go to Enrique's then. They have the most original and stunning swimsuits. You will find something at Enrique's; but they are expensive. Make sure you take your credit card. I will show you where it is after we have a bite to eat at 'Le Cirque'. The crepes there melt in your mouth.'

The crepes at Le Cirque were everything that Jade had claimed and the décor was stunning. The café/restaurant had murals on every wall that depicted the inside of a circus tent. A huge silk parachute was hung high in the ceiling. The whole café had obviously been designed with a circus theme. There were long satin sashes hanging from the high ceiling in rich reds and purples. The wall next to the bar displayed one huge mural that was reminiscent of a French street café with a man on a unicycle who had a sinewy woman on his back, her arms outstretched, her expression joyous. Couples and children sat at the wrought iron tables in the mural and the room appeared full of happy people. It was both clever and appealing Chelsea thought. Even if the room was empty it would still appear full of life. The tables in the room were the same as those in the mural carrying the theme into the dining area. It was enchanting.

Chelsea and Jade dominated the lunchtime conversation and Jack took the opportunity to observe Chelsea in yet another setting. He was surprised to see the two women develop an instant rapport, chatting about everything from fashion to childcare. Chelsea possessed such warmth and enthusiasm he couldn't imagine anyone not responding to her. If only he could get her to respond to him.

He had sensed a little guardedness in her when they had eaten at the Centrepoint restaurant and again in the car on their trip from Coolangatta, but now here with Jade she was relaxed. He wondered if the reserve towards him was due to chemistry between them. He certainly felt a zing when he was around her. He found himself drawn to whatever part of the room she inhabited. He had watched her with the cast of 'Daydream Island' and had noticed with admiration the way she had been instantly comfortable with the cast and production crew. He had noticed that she had both Gavin and Jade, laughing and responding to her. He really wanted to know how she would respond to him. Did she feel the same buzz that he did? He had to know.

Chelsea entered Enrique's full of excitement. This was another world, a world of colour and style. She had never been anywhere quite like Le Cirque and now in Enrique's she found a neutral background of muted ivory and pale toffee walls showcased the exotic colours of the rows of swimsuits. Jack and Jade had gone to her PR office and she had two hours of free time before Jack would meet her back at Le Cirque and take her to the beach house where she would spend the next week. With the $5,000 credit card from the prize in her purse she was ready for some serious shopping and a fabulous swimsuit was first on the list.

This was going to be really difficult, she thought, looking at the rows of gorgeous costumes on display. She took four into the cubicle and tried them on. Chelsea couldn't make a decision because two of the four looked great. There was a black slinky one that clung to her curves and an emerald green creation with Grecian folds that draped around her neck with silky comfort. She was just standing in the middle of the huge fitting room when the attendant, a tall elegant woman in her fifties with hair piled in a high chignon said, 'Darling, this one is you, just take a peak.'

Chelsea moaned under her breath, she was always self-conscious around clothing saleswomen. She had heard the 'this is you' line a thousand times. Nevertheless she did as she was bidden by the woman and poked her head through the lavish gold drapes. The swimming costume the woman was holding took her breath away.

It was a tiger print with the face of the tiger across the top. In beautiful tawny shades that matched her caramel hair and golden blonde highlights this swimsuit positively screamed 'Chelsea'.

She tried it on and knew her search was over. The eyes of the tiger had tiny amber diamantes and across the bust area there were tiny clear diamantes, shiny black and smoky charcoal beads. There was a line of black river pearls around the neckline that plunged between her soft round breasts. Deciding that it was time to lash out because the prize credit card only lasted for the week she also bought the emerald green costume. She couldn't resist a tropical beach bag and a pair of gold things, for practical reasons of course.

At the next shop she found a pair of sneakers that were cream canvas with de-lustred gold piping and an arrangement of amber stones on each side. At another store a halter neck dress in pale gold was just begging to go home with her. Who was she to argue, she thought with a giggle as she included a gold evening purse and a pale straw hat. She wore the sundress, glad of its cool caress after travelling. She folded her coffee linen trousers and pale yellow silk tee shirt and put them in the beach bag.

She was ready to meet Jack. She buzzed with excitement and more than a little anticipation. She told herself the butterflies in her stomach were due to the fact that she was nervous of the surf and not that she was meeting Jack.

Growing up in numerous country towns had meant she had no experience of the ocean, but even worse was the fact that her only swimming skill was an awkward dog paddle. She had never learned to breathe properly. She would have to make sure she didn't go into the surf past her ankles.

Jack saw her coming and felt a physical blow to his solar plexus. She was beautiful. She looked so young and carefree with her hair down and the pale gold dress flowing around her slim brown legs. She was all soft curves and femininity.

Chapter 7

The beach house was everything she had ever dreamed about. There was even a huge arrangement of bright dahlias on the sleek glass table in the sunroom that overlooked the ocean.

Golden rays of the sun filtered through gauzy chiffon drapes. The room was like a glass greenhouse with large leaved potted plants in the corners. The deep green leaves contrasted with the soft sage green and delicate tea rose hues of the floral mat that dominated the room. There were white cane chairs with plump sage striped cushions. The ambience was welcoming and cosy. Sliding doors opened onto the beach.

The surf was much flatter than she had imagined. Her fears of facing the raging surf abated. She could manage these waves. She had only been to Bondi Beach in Sydney a few times with friends and had been terrified of the pounding surf. Having only experienced the country she was intimidated by the surging currents. She had deliberately never watched the movie 'Jaws', because she had enough fear to contend with.

'I could almost handle that, I think' she said as she watched the mesmerizing swell of the waves.

'Quite the country mouse aren't you?' said Jack.

'Dad promised us a beach holiday every year, but it never eventuated.' She signed wistfully.

Jack was surprised that she hadn't fussed over the less than five star accommodation. He showed her around the two bedroom house. It had an open plan design and you could see the ocean from the kitchen bench. The kitchen was stocked with milk, coffee and tea. Chelsea made a mental note to buy bread rolls, cereal and fruit.

There was an indoor pool that was enclosed by glass bay windows and there was a small entertainment area with outdoor lounges and where ferns grew in lush abandon. Jade and her real estate husband must be doing well.

'This is gorgeous,' she said, eyeing the clear aqua water, 'I can practice here.'

'Practice?' queried Jack, perplexed.

'Yes, I'm afraid I am a little nervous in the water. I never really learned to swim properly.' She was hesitant, unsure. He warmed to this new vulnerable side of her.

'Well, a few swimming lessons wouldn't go astray then.'

'I'm afraid I would look a bit silly in the shallow end with floaties on my arms, learning with all the pre-schoolers.'

'That's where I come in.' His eyes were inscrutable. She sensed an undercurrent to his words. She chose to ignore it and battled to keep on even ground.

'A lawyer with swimming advice—that must be above and beyond the call of duty, are you afraid of a lawsuit if I drown?' He blanched, her words had stung him and she regretted them as soon as they were out of her mouth. Why did she always antagonize attractive men? Was it because of her father?

'No, Miss Prickly, I am not worried about a law suit.' He paused and decided on honesty. 'I like you Chelsea Prentiss; and I would like the chance to get past that wall of polite resistance that you cultivate whenever anyone says anything personal. You are warm and funny but you are as scared as hell.'

'I'm sorry,' she whispered, looking away. His eyes were compelling, she must resist them. She wanted to say more, but couldn't find the words.

'Well?' he said, folding his arms and leaning back on the door frame to the kitchenette.

She smiled a tentative smile. 'Okay. Thank you kind sir, I accept your gracious offer. I would be grateful for a little swimming coaching.'

'I'll get your bags from the car.' Jack's voice was clipped.

Chelsea sensed his withdrawal. She kicked herself for pushing him away; would she always be wary, suspicious? Jack returned and ignored the tension that had sprung up between them. He was not going to jeopardise this; he only had a week to get to know her.

'Come on, let's go for a walk. You can harass me tomorrow; you can make up more imaginative names for me. But now, we should wander down the beach and get you some more supplies from the kiosk. Are you hungry?

'I'm starving!'

'There is a great wood fire pizzeria on The Esplanade, we can sit there and watch the sunset. Think of it as research.'

Outside the twilight was gathering its grey mists into long shadows. The clouds reached down to the water and occasionally parted to let the last piercing rays of the sun triumph over the dusk with a golden blaze. The pale streaks of cloud seemed to be gathered from the spray of the ocean.

'Do you think those clouds are touching the ocean?' Chelsea

asked.

'Or perhaps the ocean is reaching up to be part of the sky?' responded Jack.

The soft scent of salt was invigorating. She was really here, she was finally having the beach holiday that she had been promised all her life. Up close the beach was amazing; it was like nothing she had ever seen. She had never been a fan of high rise buildings and urban development but the cityscape so near to the beach was breathtaking. They took off their shoes and wandered aimlessly through the gently ebbing surf. This was a quiet beach, perfect to heal Chelsea's fears. It was shallow and rippling as far out as she could see.

Occasionally a small wave curled up to her knees. Chelsea squealed in delight as she stepped back into Jack's waiting arms. At last, he thought as he closed his arms around her. She did not resist, merely turning to reward him with an open joyful smile.

He drew her closer. Chelsea blushed. She is radiant, thought Jack. They continued walking and Jack threaded his fingers through hers. Chelsea's heart hammered and warmth crept through her veins. Somehow the simple touch of hands seemed more intimate than any other gesture could have been. It seemed so natural, heart responding to heart.

'You are not going to keep calling me Swamp Creature are you? Is it your revenge?'

'Revenge? Never!' he intoned trying to keep a straight face, 'Whatever would I want revenge for, surely not the insult of being likened to a car hoist, a ham sandwich or Japanese paper folding— and what was that other one...? Ah yes, Stretch. Why on earth would a man want revenge for that?'

Chelsea smiled, he was teasing her.

'No, I am not going to call you Swamp Creature, I have a much better name for you,' he said with a smirk.

'I can't wait,' said Chelsea, crossing her arms in mock indignation. 'This should be good.'

'It is. Has anyone ever told you that you have a story for everything and everyone? You're like the Sultan's bride in Arabian Nights—Scheherazade. You are my Scheherazade. That fits perfectly, after all that's where I first saw you, in the Arabian Nights tent at the Harbour Bridge.'

Her heart skipped a beat and she forgot to breathe. 'Well, I guess that's an improvement on Swamp Creature at least.' She laughed. 'I suppose I will have to stop calling you a ham sandwich. What would you like me to call you?'

'Ooh I don't know, how about 'irresistible'? You could try that for a start,' he suggested, his eyes alight with humour, 'or darling, that always has a nice ring to it.'

'In your dreams, Stretch.' She laughed; a warm sultry sound.

'I would rather be in *your* dreams, my sweet Scheherazade.' His grey eyes were inscrutable. He did not pull her into his arms for a passionate embrace but instead took her hand again. He is not like other men, thought Chelsea, he doesn't press for every advantage, seize every opportunity. Either he is a careful player, or he reads me well. She wondered which; either way she was in trouble.

It was his very reserve, his quiet assessment of her that Chelsea found so appealing. Whether by clever artifice or natural intuition this man was in tune with her. It was both disconcerting and tantalizing. He was the waltz to her tango.

They carried the wood fire pizza back to the beach house sunroom with its white cane love seats. They tore the cardboard box into pieces and used it as plates for the pizza. They feasted on its succulent richness as the sun finally deserted the night sky, bequeathing them a whisper of breeze. They shared a piquant white wine and grew mellow.

'Why do you keep men at arm's length?' he questioned when

they had relaxed into the cushions of the cane chairs.

'I'm short sighted, they look better at that distance. Anyway I try to be democratic about it; I also discriminate against small yappy dogs, warring old men and irritable budgerigars.'

'Oh, I really am in fine company aren't I? It won't work you know, I *will* get closer to you. What are you going to do about that, Scheherazade?' he said relaxing back into the billowing softness of the lounge with a satisfied smirk, his eyes closed.

'I guess I will just have to get longer arms.' She threw a cushion at his head and was surprised when his lithe arm snaked out to catch it.

'Of course, I will only ever be as close as you want me, you will have to ask.' A shiver went through her. Coming from anyone else this would have seemed supreme arrogance but Jack's eyes glinted darkly in the moonlight and she realised that he meant every word he said. The fire in his eyes hinted that he wanted her very much, but the decision was hers.

Chelsea felt a frisson of fear. If Jack had been the kind of aggressor that every other man had been she would have run a mile but the sensual tug of his patient seduction was bringing her undone. He was outside of her experience. She retreated into herself. The longer she kept him at a distance, the longer her heart would be safe.

'So I will have to request you, will I? Do you want that signed and dated, in triplicate, counsellor?'

'No, for you I will make an exception. Once, once will do nicely thank you. Sealed with a kiss. Just your sweet lips on mine.'

Chelsea sucked in a ragged breath.

Jack changed tack again immediately and began to make plans for the next day. Chelsea's head was spinning. So much for having the upper hand with him. She was a wreck. She walked him to the hire car and he held her shoulders tenderly, placing a warm lingering kiss on her forehead.

It was many hours before Chelsea could sleep and when she did she saw his eyes, and felt his burning lips on her forehead again. She was still asleep when the doorbell rang the next morning. Moaning softly she padded to the door in bare feet and was stunned to see a small girl about six or seven years of age standing there with purple zinc on her nose and a jaunty hat.

'I'm Jemima, you must be Chelsea, that's a funny name, hurry up Uncle Jack, men are so slow, don't you think?'

The early morning sprite had already walked in the front door and was standing hand on hip eyeing Jack and Chelsea. She brushed back her long straight hair in frustration at the adults in her life and then threw herself onto the sofa with a world weary sigh.

Chelsea looked at her watch and couldn't believe that it was already nine in the morning. Jack had made plans to pick her up and take her to the studio at this time and she was still rubbing the sleep from her eyes. She guessed that the sprite who had introduced herself with such confidence was Jade's daughter. She had her mother's generous rosy lips and huge dramatic eyes. Jade had talked about her children at lunch.

'Slight change of plans, sorry,' said Jack as he came up the driveway from parking the car. 'Jamie has had complications after surgery and Jade asked me to have Jem.'

'I wanted to go to the television studio to see what all the nonsense is about for that show you are going to be on, but Uncle Jack said we are going to Sea World,' piped up Jemima.

'Sounds marvellous,' said Chelsea with audible relief, looking to Jack for confirmation. He gave her a slight nod. His eyes were anxious.

'How is Jamie?' she questioned.

'They have put him on intravenous antibiotics; he had quite a few doses through the night. Jade and Andrew are with him now. But he will be fine, won't he, sugar plum?' picking Jem up and throwing her over his shoulder. She giggled loudly.

'Put me down Uncle Jack, you'll break your back.' This statement was the excuse to start a rhyme, a game that Chelsea was soon to discover could go on for hours.

'I made a poem! Uncle Jack with a broken back, he'll need to hit the sack with his broken back. Don't go down the track, Uncle Jack with a broken back.' Jem let out a shrill laugh that had Chelsea scurrying to her room to get some beach things together.

'That voice is a lethal weapon,' she murmured to Jack as they sat in the air conditioned comfort of the hire car and set out for Waterworld.

'We are having an adventure,' chirped Jem, 'do you like adventures, Chelsea?'

'*Oh, I do Jem.* I try to fit one in every day before breakfast,' laughed Chelsea.

'You're funny, Chelsea, you *can't* have an adventure *every* day. That would be *too too* much,' said Jem, 'I am glad you are coming on our adventure. At least you get ready faster than Uncle Jack. I had to jump on him three times to make him wake up this morning.'

Chelsea had imagined Jack staying in one of the luxury hotels and it took a slight adjustment to think of him being woken by a rowdy niece. It seemed so normal and ordinary. It made him seem so much more human. He was obviously close to his sister's family.

Jem soon nodded off to sleep in the back with her head resting on her doll. Jack told Chelsea that she didn't have to be on set for the next two days and her time was her own.

'I can be your tour guide if you like,' he said.

'I like,' Chelsea said simply.

The lawyer in Jack Devon had decided to take the day off,

Chelsea discovered as they went from attraction to attraction. She didn't know whether it was the presence of Jemima that unleashed the child within but she decided that she liked this side of him. It certainly took any previous tension that had been between them out of the situation and allowed her to totally relax.

Jemima hopped and skipped, twirled and chatted nonstop all day. It was obvious that she adored her Uncle Jack and Chelsea could see why. They visited Pirate Cove. Jemima screamed with joy when she saw the tall palms and the clear aqua water. From that moment Jack became Jack Sparrow, from the mincing walk to the extravagant head turning and the languid hand gestures. He was hilarious.

'You certainly hammed it up when you saw Pirate Cove with the pirate ship,' remarked Chelsea, 'who knew that under that brisk businesslike façade lay a failed actor.'

'I take exception to that, many lawyers have become great actors.' countered Jack.

Jem snatched Jack's hand, 'We just *have* to go to the waterslides, Uncle Jack, they are *the* best!' Even though Jemima declared she wanted to go on the adults' waterslide Jack insisted on going to the junior one. Chelsea had never had so much fun in one day in her life. She realised that fun had been in short supply in her life and was grateful to Jack for adding playfulness into the day.

They slid down on the stomach, on their backs and all together, sometimes with Jemima sandwiched between them and sometimes in front waving her arms and loudly declaring herself to be the captain of the universe. Jack thought how perfect it was to have Chelsea's warm body wrapped around him squealing in delight, holding on to him for dear life. The excuse of having Jemima had given him the perfect opportunity to get close to Chelsea without frightening her away and he was relishing it.

Jemima decided that she was the boss of all the activities and

Jack was pleased to take her mind off her sick brother. She waited in the shallow pool at the bottom of the slide and insisted that Jack and Chelsea come down together lying down so they would go really fast like some of the teenage boys were doing in the extreme waterslide.

Jack didn't need to be told twice and holding Chelsea firmly between his legs he set off with her, but half way down he slowed to a stop bracing their descent with his legs. Slowly turning Chelsea to face him he gave her quick searing kiss before turning her back and flying down the slide. They hit the cold water at the bottom and Chelsea swung around and attempted to throw an angry remark but it came out with a giggle, 'I thought you were going to make me ask, counsellor?'

'I didn't say *all the time*', said Jack beaming at his cleverness, 'you didn't read the fine print.'

'Silly me,' said Chelsea, 'arguing with a lawyer.'

'Yes, I would have thought you had more sense,' he parried.

'Well, you should have more self-control,' she quipped.

'I have exercised extreme and fabulous self-control all day. Even though I have been indecently provoked by a beautiful woman, in a sexy green bathing suit, I have not once called you a swamp creature.' His eyes were triumphant.

On the trip home Jemima was just as excited as she had been all day and joined Jack when he sang his own pirate version of 'I am Jack Sparrow, I live on a boat narrow, I need a wheelbarrow.' to the tune of 'Alive Alive O.'

'You can't have a wheelbarrow on a pirate ship, Uncle Jack,' protested Jemima.

'But I need a wheelbarrow to rhyme with Sparrow,' argued Jack.

'But Uncle Jack where would you put a wheelbarrow on a pirate ship?' questioned Jemima.

'I would keep it in the ship's hold and store all my marrows,' he supplied helpfully. Jemima giggled and joined another rousing chorus that included Jack Sparrow's marrows. This time Chelsea joined in figuring that if she couldn't beat them she might as well join them.

'But Uncle Jack, nobody takes marrows on a pirate ship,' corrected Jemima.

'Oh, but you are wrong my dear, the best pirates in the world never leave port without at least a ton of marrows,' Jack claimed in haughty wounded tones.

'But Uncle Jack...'

'Jemima, you know...' Chelsea began.

'I know, never argue with a lawyer,' finished Jemima, 'Mummy says it all the time when Uncle Jack is around.'

After tea Jemima was still wound up and showed no sign of slowing down. Just after tea Jade rang to tell them that Jamie had been taken back to theatre to have an abscess drained that had formed after his surgery. Jade and Andrew would wait at the hospital for him to come out of theatre. Jack offered to take Jemima home and care for her but Jemima clung to Chelsea with wide eyed concern.

Chelsea took charge just as she would have down at the preschool. She told Jack that she would be fine with Jemima and when Jemima said, 'I want Captain Sparrow too' Chelsea simply said, 'Why not, we sleep on a pirate's ship tonight, me hearties!'

They reinvented the glassed sunroom and Chelsea had Jack carry out the king size mattress from the master bedroom. Putting Jemima on the mattress Chelsea put soft music on and they all watched the sunset. Jemima lay between them snuggled into Chelsea with her head resting on Chelsea's lap. The gentle strains of orchestra music tinkled in the background. Chelsea softly drew a light finger along Jemima's eyelids as she slowly drifted into sleep.

'That's a fabulous trick, you must try that on me sometime,' whispered Jack sensuously over Jemima's tousled head.

'She was overtired,' explained Chelsea, 'we do that at the preschool all the time.'

'Where is this preschool? I want to enrol in a preschool where a gorgeous woman lies down beside me with my head in her lap and caresses my eyes to put me to sleep.'

'In your dreams, Stretch.'

'I would rather be in yours, Scheherazade.'

Chelsea moaned in defeat, she wasn't even going to try to have the last word. She drifted into a sleep to a world with pirates, marrows and Jack.

Chapter 8

'Mummy, Mummy!' squealed Jemima. 'We slept on a pirate ship and Jack was Captain Jack Sparrow the Pirate King with a ship full of marrows.'

Good grief, thought Jack as he opened one reluctant eye to see his sister and Chelsea sitting at the breakfast bar chatting over coffee and an energetic Jemima running around the room. He moaned and put the pillow over his head. He was sure he hadn't slept a wink. Being in the same bed with Chelsea had been a frustrating enough to be so close but so far. He hadn't counted on sleeping on a breezy patio with his energetic niece who made strange noises in her sleep and slapped him.

'Your child,' he boomed at Jade, 'snores appallingly and is a violent sleeper.'

'Welcome to my world,' replied Jade.

Jamie had come through the second surgery well and after collecting Jemima's clothes and books Jade took her to the hospital to see her brother, thanking Chelsea with warmth.

'What about me?' complained Jack, 'I helped.'

'What about you!' answered Jade as she shooed Jemima out the door amid claims of undying love for Chelsea and adding in her best grown up voice, 'We must do lunch.'

Jack groaned, 'Just like her mother, just like her both her aunties. Growing up with women was a severe strain. Don't know how I survived to tell the tale.'

'They probably spoiled you rotten,' said Chelsea avoiding looking at Jack sitting shirtless opposite her at the breakfast bar with his normally tidy hair ruffled and dark stubble on his chin. He was drop dead gorgeous even if he was pretending to be tired and cranky. She bustled noisily around the kitchen to avoid looking at him.

'Crucifixion would have been easier,' moaned Jack determined to remain the martyr.

'So you don't like mornings?' laughed Chelsea.

'Coffee! Now; woman!' he demanded banging his mug on the breakfast bar.

Chelsea demurred letting out of peal of laughter that caught in Jack's chest. It was the most beautiful morning sound he had heard for a long time.

'What's on the itinerary for today, pirate and tour guide?' she questioned lightly her heart thumping.

'Swimming lessons, wench.'

Chelsea went to the master bedroom and changed into her new tiger skin bathers. When she arrived at the pool Jack was already there.

He was in the shallow end and he had tried to squeeze into a pair of floaties. Chelsea bit her lip so that she wouldn't laugh out loud. The floaties only came to his elbows. He was mocking her but his benign face betrayed nothing.

The tiger skin bathers moulded her curves. Jack's throat constricted. Chelsea smiled; a dazzling smile.

'Alright, I get it, you've had your fun, now I will be the perfect pupil, I promise,' she said, saluting him extravagantly.

The water was cool and sensuous on her skin. Jack began by getting her to relax and put both hands on the side of the pool and put her face in the water but she was still tense.

'Okay, we will try something more basic,' he said, calming her fears. 'Lie back in the water and float.' She was still anxious but did as he had bidden. She sucked in air and sank; her head slipping below the water. She erupted from the water, coughing and spluttering. Jack stood behind her, looped his arms through hers cradling her shoulders and lowered her into the water, resting her body on his. She drew in a nervous breath and so did Jack but for very different reasons. Desire shot through him like fire. He struggled for control. This woman deserved time. He would wait until he knew she desired him as much as he desired her.

With her body resting on Jack's Chelsea finally began to relax and breathe normally. Jack kept up a stream of quiet reassurances until he felt all of the tension leave her body. When they had drifted in the pool for a while he told her to kick her legs and with her body still resting on him he kicked gently with her and steered them around the pool.

If I had known swimming lessons were like this, thought Chelsea, I would have taken them up years ago. Her body responded to his nearness with a zing both familiar and new. She had never felt so attracted to a man before. It was his quiet reserve that allowed her to relax and respond. The other men in her life had been so busy with their words and charm that she had felt under threat. But this man with his discerning eyes, gentle touch and warm humour was bringing her undone like no other had done.

He was humming, how disarming, Chelsea thought. She strained to make out the melody. It sounded suspiciously like a bawdy pirate ballad. She smiled.

Jack took her hands in his and began to teach her a slow rhythmic backstroke. As their entwined arms reached above their heads her face caressed his stubbly chin. His loins stirred. He changed tack. He needed distance.

She moved away. She needed distance.

She was relieved when he wanted her to practice floating by on her own and she was surprised to find that it was far easier than it had been at the beginning. He made her kick with her head down and a flotation board in front of her.

I miss his touch, she thought. He is too far away.

This is harder than I expected, she is too far away, he thought.

'Have you learned CPR, 'resuss'?' he questioned. *I need to hold her again.*

Jack showed her the posters on the ABC of resuscitation and explained them. His voice was like warm honey. Who would have thought that Airway, Breathing, and Circulation could sound sexy? He made her lay on the side of the pool while he held deft fingers under her chin to show her the right angle to hold the jaw for respiratory resuscitation, the 'kiss of life'. His gentle breath teased her face. He came close to her mouth and counted her breathing but did not claim her lips. Don't get too close she willed. He moved away. Come back and kiss me, her wayward heart begged.

Then he lay by the pool and taught her how to hold his jaw at the right angle and watch for the rise and fall of his chest that would tell her she was getting air into his lungs. Her breath tickled his face. Kiss me now, his eyes begged. She repaid the favour, taunting him with her closeness. Their breath mingled. Their eyes met. She withdrew. Jack threw himself into the cool water of the pool.

Her eyes followed him.

'What do I do when someone is in trouble in the water?' she asked.

I am in trouble in the water, he thought.

'You take air to them,' he said, enjoying the confusion in her eyes.

'You're playing with me,' she said. Play with me some more.

'Saving a life is serious business,' he said, his eyes hooded, his emotions hidden.

'Then how?'

'Pretend you're drowning and I will show you,' he said.

She laughed and jumped in. She sank deep under the water and thrashed around as he had said. She couldn't believe that only an hour ago she had been afraid to be under the water.

His powerful arms were around her holding her under the water. Her eyes opened in shock. His eyes locked on hers. Trust me, they said, as his lips claimed hers. A small panic rose and was washed away with the sensuous press of his soft lips and her body surrendered to his firm embrace. He breathed air into her mouth, filling her lungs; she accepted the warm saving breath.

They rose to the surface and burst through the water gasping and laughing. 'Do people really do that?' she gurgled joyfully, her arms wrapped around his neck.

'If they don't, they should,' he responded, his warm laugh tickling the soft willing curve of her neck.

He drew her closer. She wound her legs around his firm torso. His eyes flared. She pressed her softness into his hard body. He held her to him, no further, no closer. Then he swept her in circles around him, spinning her closer. Her eyes begged. He waited for the words.

'Say what you want. What do you want Chelsea?' he breathed, his voice low.

'I want you, Jack.'

'What do you want me to do Chelsea?' he purred her name. The intensity of his eyes left no mistakes. He wanted no misunderstanding.

'Just kiss me Jack. Now.' Her arms snaked around his neck. She pulled him closer. Her fingers caressed the dark stubble on his chin. She touched his lips, inviting, welcoming, causing him to suck in a ragged breath.

He resisted her urgency and began a slow sensual assault. His eyes roved her lush curves but always returned to her love drenched eyes for confirmation. His firm lips followed his gentle exploring hands. He concentrated on building her desire for him. He had to have her willing, without regret, fully his own.

His eyes asked the question. Her eyes answered yes. He carried her to the master bedroom, cradling her against his warm hungry body. His unhurried enjoyment of her body allowed her passion to flower to full blossom. Unchained by his selfless focus on her pleasure she abandoned herself to him. His hands and body delivered what his eyes had promised. His lingering kisses had been an adequate prelude to the symphony of her heart.

'Chelsea...'

'Jack...' they began together, then laughed.

'I want you to stay,' she said, her eyes soft with longing. 'Stay here with me. I want to wake up with you in the morning. If you want to make love to me again, I need you to stay.'

'I couldn't have said it better myself,' murmured Jack, the yearning in his eyes matching hers. 'Well, I probably could have, but I don't like to show off this early in the day.'

They made love again in the sunroom of the beach house while the noonday sun was gloriously ruling the sky.

'We have this week,' murmured Chelsea to his chest, 'and then...'

'And then...' responded Jack seeking her lips once more. You will be mine. He didn't say the words yet but Jack Devon had never been surer of anything in his life. He would give her time. He would give her himself. He had always known what he wanted and worked hard to get it, and now he wanted the feisty adorable woman in his arms.

Chelsea had been waiting for an hour on set for the action to begin. Jade had picked her up from the beach house and would call back for her in a few hours. She had been introduced to the writers and some of the production and camera crew. Jade had told her that they would be filming the scene that she had written today and that she would be there for publicity photos.

She was fast becoming aware that television studios were not the glamorous places that most people assumed they were. The production crew were the only ones who seemed to be active as a woman with a blue tooth headset, was busily given instructions to the camera crew and talking on the phone at the same time.

'Hello. My name is Sophie Stanton. I'm the producer. You must be Chelsea,' said the woman with the headset. She wore sleek black slacks and a fitted blue striped shirt and wore her black hair in a short style that would have been severe on someone else, but Sophie was a stunning woman and could carry it off. Chelsea had been watching her for some time and was amazed at her energy and enthusiasm. She was vibrant. Chelsea could imagine her at the preschool keeping up with the energetic toddlers and pre-schoolers.

'Yes, I'm Chelsea.' Chelsea returned the firm handshake offered to her.

'Did Jade fill you in on today?'

'She said you were filming the scene I wrote,' replied Chelsea.

'Good, that's great we are ready to go, so buckle up.' With that cheerful remark Sophie became all business again.

The set in front of Chelsea was the lavish kitchen of Blair and

Brittany's townhouse. One of the production crew arrived and placed a huge vase of fresh flowers on the breakfast bar. This was going to be used by Blair to put the fire out when Brittany casually used a cigarette lighter to set Blair's newspaper on fire. They had already filmed the scenes that would be used as the reminiscences of Brittany where she would think back and remember that she had put the electric blanket on high and accidentally cooked Blair's romantic dinner with disinfectant because she had tried to do it by candlelight. Today's scene would be the final touch to that drama.

Susan Ells who played Brittany arrived in a loose silk dressing gown that just skimmed her knees. The cameraman who had been languidly standing around became snapped into action instantly and when the director arrived everything flowed smoothly and professionally. Chelsea was amazed at Susan's focus and dedication. She was certainly nothing like the frothy socialite that she portrayed. If she thought the scene she was playing was mundane no one would have known by her demeanour.

The camera followed Brittany as she waited tensely for Blair to come home from the gym and join her in the kitchen. She wistfully gazed out of the window and sat for long minutes while the camera filmed her pausing to remember the past few days and her numerous attempts to get her husband's attention.

When Blair's key was heard in the lock she tensed and was instantly alert. Gavin arrived on set as Blair and filled the set with his personality. After a nonchalant peck on Brittany's cheek he settled to read the paper and drink the beer he had taken from the fridge, ignoring the coffee that Brittany had made for him. Brittany fumed as he also ignored her. After a frigid silence she leant forward and very calmly and deliberately flicked the cigarette lighter at the bottom of his newspaper. It was a few tense moments before Blair realised that his newspaper was on fire. He hurled the flaming paper down on the bench and picking up the nearby vase threw the water and the flowers over the paper and Brittany. She screamed in horror and ran from the room as the director called, 'That's a wrap, well done people.'

Gavin came over to Chelsea and kissed her on the cheek, 'Hello my sweet, how did you like it?'

'You were fabulous darling, I'm actually impressed.'

'Which means you weren't expecting to be,' said Gavin sagely.

'Not really, I wasn't sure that what I wrote would translate well to the actual real life action, but you two made it really come to life.'

'You writers are just as insecure as the rest of us, aren't you my sweet?'

Susan arrived back on set and was now dressed in jeans and a white T shirt with 'I'm not a diva' in gold letters on the front. She had her hair back in a ponytail and looked more like a teenager than the competent singer and actor that she was. She welcomed Chelsea warmly and joined her and Gavin and Sophie for a coffee break.

Sophie had hardly sat down when she was back on the phone firing rapid instructions. She excused herself, leaving her coffee to get cold.

The camera crew was already moving to another area for the next scene and the studio was alive with staff. Chelsea felt a little in the way and was relieved to see Jack waiting at the doorway in casual chinos and a short sleeved chambray shirt. Jade must have been held up again but Chelsea didn't mind. She wanted every minute she could have with Jack.

Hours later with Jacks arms around her even the surf felt like a friend instead of an ancient foe that had called to her with its tempting strength, mocking her fears. They frolicked like dolphins, carefree and young.

The exercise and the salt air had made them starving and they ate savoury buttery croissants from the corner bakery and ate them on the walk home.

Jack allowed her into his world. He talked about the kind of work he did and the punishingly long hours; the overseas travel.

The wind began to blow, long rough and hard; moaning softly through the shutters. Lightning flashed and a charcoal darkness descended. They were cocooned in the house. They sat in the patio watching the wind whipping the waves relentlessly while the rain thudded the roof with metallic rhythm. They drank hot chocolate, enjoying each other and the pounding sounds of the storm outside. They played board games buying and selling properties, laughing and talking as if they were old friends.

When the storm lulled and the darkness was still thick and heavy Jack put a CD on and the sultry sounds of saxophone blues played in the background while they lay on the thick carpet on the huge lounge cushions wrapped in each other's arms.

'I think there were a lot of advantages for you growing up in a house full of women,' said Chelsea, caressing his stubbly jaw line.

'How do you figure that?'

'It has made you more aware. You are very comfortable around women. You're used to our moods and secrets.'

'No man ever gets used to that. And I got precious few secrets from my sisters. To this day I dream of slamming bedroom doors.' Chelsea laughed. 'To the older two I was a pest and to Kylie I was the brother that was supposed to get her out of trouble and introduce her to my friends.'

'Well as least you didn't have the burden of being the eldest and held responsible for everyone,' said Chelsea.

'It must have been hard on you when your father left,' said Jack, threading his fingers through the hair at the nape of her neck.

'At least he came to visit often enough. We never had to pine for him. It was hard on mum because she had to scrape for every cent, I don't know what would have happened to us if it hadn't been for Nana Greerson.'

'But he let you all down. I guess that's why it is hard for you to trust. I can understand that. Even though I was 21 when mum and dad divorced it hits you hard. You just expect that they will be together forever.'

'I think I did a good job of hiding my pain when I was a child. I thought I had to be strong for mum. She was very loving and warm but she wasn't really a fighter. And they never really explained what happened. When you are a child you wonder if their leaving had something to do with you. As you grow up you know it isn't about you but that sense of insecurity remains at some level.' Chelsea rested back into his arms.

'So you never asked questions?'

'Not really, if you sense that your parent can't cope with the situation you don't want to add your own emotions to their burden. Mind you Alicia asked enough questions for everyone. But they were such angry questions and mum retreated even more. We never asked dad anything because we were afraid we would see even less of him.'

'It was easier on me because I had left home. At Uni parents weren't exactly on the most talked about list. Anyway Scott and I hung out at Geraldine's. She lectured and smothered us enough for several parents.'

'I had a world of old ladies in Tamworth. I must have been the most adored afternoon tea guest in the street. Other kids had paper runs and I had meals on wheels except that I was the one getting fed by them!'

'So you're not just the Pied Piper of children, you collect old ladies too.' Jack could just picture her riding her bike around the neighbourhood.

'There was one gorgeous old dear who lived opposite Ezzie. She lived in the last house on the street. She played the piano beautifully and had three huge cats. I remember the first time I went to see her I didn't know where to sit because the cats were sitting on all the armchairs.'

Jack laughed, 'What did you do?'

'I just stood and waited to see what the old lady would do. She gave the cats a severe talking to about their manners when guests were over and they stretched regally and went outside with their noses in the air. It was such a shock to me because we weren't allowed to sit in our Nana's lounge chairs as children and visit a place where the cats had pride of place was marvellous indeed.'

'You have led a rich and colourful life, Scheherazade.'

'I know. I am so well-travelled,' she said with a laugh. Jack compared his own overseas travel and realised that he probably couldn't remember much about the places he had been. His visits had been hectic business trips. He admired Chelsea's capacity to enjoy life.

Chapter 9

The vibe on set should have been electric. It was anything but that. Chelsea had learned over the past few days during her time on the set of the soap opera that the work environment was very businesslike and official. It was very different than what she had imagined. The elaborate sets were not always in magnificent homes as they appeared on screen but were often corners of the studio. Several homes were used for much of the action but there were usually more technical staff on set than actors.

She suspected that some of the cast saw her as less than welcome, certainly Emma did; she was a civilian in the rarefied world of their creativity. She understood that sentiment and fervently wished she was elsewhere herself. She had come in to see if she was needed the next day as she did every afternoon. She had really spent very little time at the studio.

Today it seemed like all the actors were on the set. There was a party scene that was to be filmed at the on screen home of Blair and Brittany; played by Gavin and newcomer Susan Ells. The actors involved were rushing around with glamorous party clothes. The air was thick with requests and complaints. Gavin was charming as always, kissing Chelsea and shaking Jack's hand.

'It's not always like this darling, usually there are only two huge egos to massage but today is a positive nightmare, not at all like it seems on the telly,' he explained. He had a towel around his neck and carried a champagne flute with pale gold liquid. 'I would offer you some, my dears but it is just cold tea, after this shoot I plan to hijack the real stuff and get seriously sloshed.' Then he was off to find his co-star and on screen wife.

Chelsea was pleased to discover that she wasn't needed until the next day when they were filming at Le Cirque the café that she had lunched in with Jack and Jade. She was more than thrilled to leave and spend the evening with Jack at the beach house. As promised he had acquired some DVD's of the soap and showed them to Chelsea so she knew the threads of the story.

They awoke late the next morning in a tangle of sheets and limbs. They had to race to the café for the scene that was Chelsea's responsibility for the prize. She was an extra and was relieved to be getting that out of the way. Jade was there with the advertising team and Jemima. They had allowed Jemima to be with Chelsea for the scene. Jemima was a dither of childish nerves but Chelsea was amazed at the change in her for the filming. Jemima acted like a complete professional and impressed everyone. They were only required to sit in the corner and sip iced chocolates laden with whipped cream.

After the filming was over some of the actors stayed and chatted, losing that glazed over expression that said they had been accosted by too many fans and exhausted by the stress of the recent on-set tension. They relaxed and chatted and Chelsea felt the ice was thawing towards her.

The artist was there painting another wall of the mural. After the lunchtime rush the café was closed to the public so that the artist could take photos of the cast in preparation to adding them to the café mural. Even the stars of the show attended then and Gavin arrived larger than life, filling the room. He was relaxed and urbane; a thorough professional.

The chatter was lively and upbeat. The mood had lifted from the previous days. Chelsea and Jack were accepted as part of the crew and Jade was always a welcome guest as she organised the PR and advertising for the show.

Jade had a huge bag of costumes from the local costume hire centre and she chatted brightly to the artist. The atmosphere was elevated to party status when the actors, Chelsea, Jack, Jade and Jemima were all given a choice of outfit. The idea was to have the actors fit in with the circus theme and their colourful images would become part of the mural and part of the local history.

The costumes all had a carnival appeal and predictably Jack chose a pirate costume. He wore a cheeky smile and a tilted black pirate hat but insisted on wearing the eye patch on his forehead complaining it made him dizzy over his eye.

Jemima pronounced him a sook, patting him patronizingly on the head. She was dressed in a pale lime and gold fairy outfit and was happily ensconced on his lap. To prove what a man he was he allowed Emma to put heavy black eye liner on. Chelsea was very relieved that she wasn't subjected to Emma's ministrations again; or torture as she had declared so vehemently to Jack.

Chelsea was interested to see that Emma's attitude to Jack was quite different than it was to her. Emma chatted and sighed and preened for him obviously impressed with a handsome man with debonair charm. Jack milked his Jack Sparrow routine for all it was worth and Chelsea felt a stab of jealousy as Emma pulled out all the stops to flirt with him. Just as Chelsea started to withdraw to protect herself, Jack's arm snaked out and he included her in his warm embrace. Relieved she relaxed back into his arms.

Emma chose a gypsy outfit that combined bold burgundy with black and silver. Chelsea waited until the cast made their selection and she was left with the choice between a leotard for the trapeze or a pencil thin suit of red white and blue stripes for the human cannon ball. She chose the red, white and blue suit and was gratified when it fit snugly. There was a top hat in electric blue with stars all over it to complete the outfit. Spirits were high in the staff room of the café where the women changed into their costumes.

When she stepped into the room Jack couldn't take his eyes of her. She even looked good in a crazy suit. The top was sleeveless and showed her sun-kissed arms. One side of the top was cobalt blue and the other was vibrant red with a high white collar that sat under her chin and revealed a little of the soft curves of her breasts. Her eyes were bright and she wore the jaunty hat with panache.

Dance music was throbbing and some of the actors were dancing. Jack glided to Chelsea's side and claimed her for the dance. Emma joined the dancers and started to jive.

'Oh baby,' sighed Gavin theatrically, 'Jiggle that jelly.'

'Shut up, Gavin,' spat Emma.

'If the corset fits, my sweet.'

Emma shot him a poisonous glare. The animosity between the two was obvious. It sounded like a relationship gone bad to Chelsea; 'hell hath no fury like a woman scorned'. But that didn't make sense; Chelsea would bet her last dollar that Gavin was gay. When she had noticed him watching one of the cameramen he had a decidedly predatory look and when she had commented that the guy was some fine eye candy Gavin had responded with 'yeah baby.'

He was so much like her brother Mitch who had only recently 'come out' to family and friends. Mitch had been greatly disappointed at the family reaction. He had been expecting fireworks and tears and everyone had just said, 'tell us something we don't know.' He had pretended to be seriously crushed that everyone had seen through his teenage attempts to be macho. When he expressed his disappointment in them for not coming up with a better response Chelsea had simply said, 'Which is precisely why we have always known Mitch, you're a diva!'

Emma was sitting on a bar stool by the window and Chelsea saw the longing look she threw at Gavin's back as he danced cheek to cheek with one of the young actresses. Chelsea went over and sat on the stool next to her. She decided on the direct approach.

'One way love kills, right?' Her voice was soft and low, conveying her compassion.

'We were so close,' Emma sighed as the dam of her emotions broke. 'We did everything together and when the downstairs of his flat flooded because his roommate left the bath running I let him stay with me.' Scalding tears coursed down her face as she relived the pain. 'I hoped he would stay, you know. We were just getting on so well. He was always so thoughtful and so affectionate, bringing tea home...oh damn, I promised myself I wouldn't cry over him again.'

'So he baulked at taking things to the next level?' Chelsea pried gently.

'Baulking doesn't begin to describe it, *he* was indignant; he said that *he* was disappointed, that he thought I understood him better than anyone. What a mess?'

'And you didn't understand anything,' supplied Chelsea.

'Nothing,' affirmed Emma, 'men expect us to be mind readers. What I really hated was that now he treats me like a leper; as if I am the one who wronged him. I guess he couldn't handle me. I thought at least we could be friends.'

'It's hard when two people want different things from a relationship,' commented Chelsea, her mind whirring. She looked over at Gavin who was dancing with another starlet making the young girl laugh in response to his over the top antics.

'Emma?' Chelsea hesitated.

'Yes, what?'

'Did you ever think that perhaps...' Emma grabbed Chelsea's arm and her eyes were like lasers.

'Think what? Come on, spill girlfriend,' her hand was like a vice.

'Did you consider that Gavin might be gay?'

Emma dropped Chelsea's wrist. 'Oh they say that about every actor on the planet,' she said dismissively, then noticed Chelsea's serious eyes. 'Oh my goodness, you're serious.'

The two women were locked into a heavy conversation for a long time with many ohs from Emma. Chelsea talked about Mitch and told Emma about her conversation with Gavin over the cameraman.

'It was more of a dawning realisation with my brother,' said Chelsea. 'I couldn't put my finger on when I knew but it was as if I had always known at some level. It wasn't a shock, although Mitch would have liked to shock us.'

Emma downed the rest of her drink. She attempted to rise suddenly from the stool and clutched Chelsea for support.

'I need to talk to him.'

'Not after the number of drinks you have knocked back, you're not!' exclaimed Chelsea returning Emma to her stool and rubbing the forearm that she had gripped. 'You know you have seriously strong hands. Have you ever thought of massaging footballers for a living?'

Emma gave a wicked laugh and relaxed back. 'That might not be a bad idea; at least not many of those guys are gay.' She leant on the breakfast bar and put her head in her hands.

'I've been such an idiot haven't I? So he didn't really reject me. I need to talk to him.'

'When you sober up will be soon enough, we'll drop you home, tomorrow will be another day.'

Emma gripped her arm, gently this time.

'Thank you Chelsea. I'm sorry I've been a cow, I thought...I don't know what I thought.'

'Rule number one for tonight,' said Chelsea firmly, 'No more thinking for you.'

Emma smiled a shy smile, 'Something tells me there is a rule number two?'

'Stop grabbing my arm, or I'll have to sue for damages and I know just the guy to handle my case.'

They both turned to look at the subject of that remark. Jack was sitting with Jem on his knee and she was playing with his pirate's beard. The memory of his kisses warmed Chelsea's body. Unconsciously she touched her lips as her eye's caught Jack's intense gaze.

'That boy can handle my case anytime, mm-mm,' said Emma.

'Rule number three...' said Chelsea.

'Don't tell me! Leave your man alone!' muttered Emma rolling her big brown eyes.

Chelsea was glad to see Emma's spirits improve but there would be one huge hangover lying in wait for her in the morning.

Jack and Chelsea walked through the late afternoon swimmers to the gourmet pizza café on the boardwalk. It was becoming their evening pattern. Jack tore the top of the cardboard pizza box in two, giving Chelsea half and set the pizza between them. She had pineapple on her side and he watched as she picked the juicy fruit smothered in melted mozzarella and popped it into her mouth. She did the same thing every time. I could watch her eat pizza for the rest of my life, he thought.

'Have you always lived in Surfer's, I mean before you moved to Sydney?' questioned Chelsea.

'Yes, but we lived in over a dozen houses that I remember,' replied Jack. 'Mum always wanted new styles and bigger rooms. Why she didn't just redecorate I will never know.'

'At least you didn't have to change schools and constantly make new friends. That's what I hated the most. Apart from the constant packing and unpacking.'

'Mum always had removalists to do the packing and unpacking and my sisters would run around crying because we were moving.'

'Being the oldest meant that I had to do a lot of that, we wouldn't have known what removalists were. Dad was a master at packing our things; we used to tell him that he must have been a genius at jigsaw puzzles as a kid. He would hire a truck and I never knew how he fitted everything in. He actually seemed to enjoy the whole process.'

'It was hard to know what my father thought about anything. He didn't get involved much. Jade used to say that he left in the morning and never knew which house he was coming home to in the evening after work. Mum was always complaining that he didn't help, and he would just hand her his credit card. They never seemed to fight about anything. My sisters had the franchise on family conflict. Wow, it was worse when we moved because they all accused each other of stealing their clothes and jewellery because they couldn't find anything. It was days before they found all their things and then they sulked for a day or two. The silence was bliss.'

'Poor lonely male, what a testosterone drought!' laughed Chelsea.

'After we moved in to a new house I would unpack all my things straight away. Even though I was falling asleep standing up I couldn't go to bed until I had all my things put away and my trinkets lined up on the dresser,' she added.

'Obsessive compulsive huh?' teased Jack.

'I guess, my sister Alicia would go around removing any signs of the previous owners but then she would sit in the middle of our bedroom and refuse to unpack for days. Mum would give up trying to make her, she would walk in the door, sigh, and walk out again.'

'Ah, the rebel.'

'Oh yeah, she hated moving. She wouldn't speak to dad for days and when she did she was loud and angry; blaming him. It's funny really. Now she is the one who travels and has the proverbial itchy feet.'

'So you didn't mind moving then?' enquired Jack.

'I *hated* it; well, not the actual moving but the leaving behind. Leaving friends and having to make new ones and fitting in at a new school, often half way through the term. But I couldn't see the point in not trying to make the best of it. Alicia took it out on dad because it was his job we were always chasing.'

'You didn't blame him?'

'I guess not. What you be the point? It was his job. I hated when he left us but I think I have kind of blanked much of that out. Alicia was angry enough for all of us. I didn't think it made much difference we still spent about the same time with him. He wasn't around much even when he lived with us. At least when he left we put down roots and went to live with mum's mother, Nana Greerson. How I loved that house! It was next door to Leisa and it was great to come back to Tamworth and find my best friend still there. It was like we had never left. We just picked up where we left off. I had a real friend again. It felt like coming home.'

'Did your mum object to all the moving?' Jack asked.

'She didn't say, but she would look really weary. She really loved dad. She would quite literally have followed him to the ends of the earth. After he left she never remarried, and when he died she was devastated even though they had been divorced for years. Whenever dad came home with his next job that involved relocating mum would just sigh and say, 'Where to now Ted?' as if she was resigned to it. Alicia would yell and say to mum, 'Why do you let him do this to us? Why don't you just say no? We don't have to go. Dad has a choice. He doesn't care about us.'

'She sounds a bit like my dad; he just went with the flow. I do remember him saying to mum, 'You make my head spin.' Funny after dad left us, mum stopped moving. But I was in my third year of Uni then so it didn't affect me that much. Well I didn't think it did, but when I think about it, I have only moved once since then.'

'Moving around wasn't as bad as when I had to go to Sydney to hospital when I was a kid. At least when we moved house I had the family.'

'You were ill as a child?'

'Yes, I had a kidney infection and we were living on a really remote property in the outback at the time where dad was the shearer's cook. So I was sent to hospital in Sydney.'

'God, that must have been hard,' said Jack. He twisted on of Chelsea's stray curls around his fingers. He could picture a tiny girl with ringlets and brave tears. 'How old were you?'

'About ten I think. I remember being too sick and tired to take out my things. Anyway I could only take a few things with me in the air ambulance so I didn't have much.' Jack's throat constricted at the thought of Chelsea suffering. He was moved by her lack of self-pity.

Jack sensed that she didn't talk about this time of her life often and he was touched that she could share it with him. He wanted to know everything he could about her.

'What was it like being so far from home?'

'I remember getting really attached to one of the toy giraffes. It had one ear missing and I kept it with me all the time I was there. When it was time to go home I put it in my suitcase to take home but I felt so bad that it wasn't really mine and some other sick kid would need it that I put it back in the ward toy box.'

Jack didn't notice the blur of the evening pedestrian traffic along the esplanade. They were just background to this incredible woman. He watched as Chelsea tore tiny pieces of the pizza base and threw them to a seagull that was hopping expectantly at her feet. He could hear the strains of Mediterranean music coming from the open door of the pizzeria, and the gentle rhythmic lapping sounds of the ocean. He had been drawn to her from the moment he saw her but now sitting across near her and watching her everyday gestures he felt something new. She was becoming a part of his days, part of his thinking. When he was with her she was centre stage.

He was becoming familiar with the lilt of her voice, the way she always tucked her hair behind her left ear, the flash of passion in her eyes when she talked about something she believed in. How the children must love her. He could picture her with the pre-schoolers gathered around her at story time while her gentle fingers caressed them as she had done with Jemima. He was envious of the children receiving her stories, he wanted to sit at her feet and listen to her forever.

'So you weren't a teddy bear kind of kid, you loved a giraffe?' His lips curved in a teasing smile. 'Don't knock it Stretch, it was one cute giraffe. Anyway all the kids fought over the teddy bears. At least the giraffe was all mine, I took that giraffe everywhere. I slept with it tucked tightly under my chin.' She swatted his arm playfully. He let out an exaggerated 'ouch' and lay back in the chair.

'I think I am becoming jealous of a giraffe. I bet you like all the broken things in life.'

His eyes were like a child's begging for more. She had a story for everything and he just loved them all. They had finished their meal and both rose and headed for the bin at the same time. In sync.

'Maybe I do. One of our kids has cerebral palsy,' she began. Jack threaded his fingers through hers. 'He is adorable. He has blonde straight-as-sticks hair that makes him look like a punk rocker, which is deceptive because he has the sweetest nature. He is like a sack of potatoes to move but he is always smiling. He is a demon for the slippery dip. As long as you want to sit him on your lap and go, he will squeal and giggle. I guess he feels normal then, flying through the air. He can't walk, but he is only two and they are hoping he can be fitted with leg braces and get mobile later on. His mother is the eternal optimist and doesn't even seem to notice that he is different. You don't see that kind of love every day. Some of the parents seem so relieved to drop their kids off. One woman calls her daughter 'whingie' because she says she cries all day at home. She doesn't cry with us. But she can throw one hell of a tantrum.'

'Who the girl or the mother?' asked Jack.

'That's a good question, one we ask ourselves often,' said Chelsea with a laugh. She realised that she had been doing most of the talking and was suddenly shy.

'So your favourite client is a paint wielding granny with violent tendencies. Tell me about the others.'

'Most of my clients are companies not people per se.' Chelsea smiled at his choice of words.

'You even talk 'legal',' she said.

'Comes with the territory I guess—a hard habit to break.'

'I know; perils of the job. I often go into the local bank with a mixture of paint, jam and vegemite on my clothes from the pre-schoolers. One of the girls embarrassed herself at her husband's work party, by wiping food of his boss's chin.'

Jack let out a roar of a laugh.

'Remind me to stay away from your friends.'

Chapter 10

'Uncle Jack, Uncle Jack, sing me the Jack Sparrow pirate song!' chirped Jemima as she hung off her uncle's arm, as he and Chelsea came through the doorway of Jade and Andrew's home. Jade had invited them for tea. Andrew was right behind his active daughter and slapped Jack on the back and leant in for a kiss from Chelsea. He had a receding hairline and he was shorter than Jack. He had a dazzling smile and the most astonishing blue eyes that Chelsea had ever seen.

'My wife is dithering on the terrace,' he said. He picked Jemima up, throwing his laughing daughter over his shoulder. 'Don't pull Uncle Jack's arms, Jem, you'll make them as long as a gorilla's and they will drag on the floor.'

'Don't be silly, daddy,' gurgled Jemima.

Andrew took Jack and Chelsea out onto the terrace that was paved with pale terracotta tiles. There was a large oval swimming pool that had a water fountain feeding into it from the wall. The pool was at the side of the house so that the view of the Broadwater and the canals was unimpeded. One could see many magnificent homes across the winding canal. The garden at the other side of the terrace was thick with Bird of Paradise flowers, the rich blues and oranges of the plumes making a striking statement. In the centre was a large outdoor dining table that was under several large canvas sails that sheltered the whole terrace. On the table was a large bowl with rose petals and steaming seafood dishes were being organised by Jade with Jemima's enthusiastic help.

Jade was dressed very casually and had her hair up in a tortoise shell clip. She was wearing white jeans and a bright orange knit top. Chelsea was glad that she had chosen to wear her denim jeans and a handmade teal top that had bright sea creatures beaded on it. Jade went inside and brought out a fragrant curried rice dish and Andrew carried a basket with crusty French bread.

Jemima insisted on sitting next to Chelsea and wanted to investigate all the sea creatures on Chelsea's top.

'Ooh, the seahorse is my favourite Chelsea,' said Jemima as she reverently touched the luminous beading.

The food was delicious and lively chatter flowed. Jade said that she had promised not to 'talk shop' and had given Andrew strict instructions to stop her if she started. Chelsea enquired after Jamie and was pleased to hear that he was eating normally and would be allowed home in a few days.

'He must be getting well because he complained when I told him that I had hired a nurse for a few days,' said Jade, obviously relieved.

'You've made quite an impression on our princess,' remarked Andrew to Chelsea. 'Well the whole family really,' he added with a twinkle towards Jack. 'How are you enjoying your prize, so far?'

'I am really enjoying the beach, and your beach house, thank you for that, it is a dream come true for me.'

'I gather that being part of the soap opera isn't part of that dream come true,' said Andrew.

'It isn't as bad as I thought. Because of the hotel fire I haven't had to be there as much as they planned, which suits me just fine. I don't think the actors are too pleased with having a 'civilian' on set. The prize wasn't their idea and I don't blame them for feeling a bit put out,' said Chelsea.

'I hear you had a run-in with a massage chair, some green gunk and a cranky make-up artist,' Andrew said. Chelsea moaned.

Jack was only too pleased to tell the story of Chelsea's narrow escape and the heroic part he had played in her rescue. He had everyone at the table in stitches including Chelsea as he mimicked her desperate attempts to flee. He had her down pat, right up to the falling towel, the arm waving and the hasty swiping to remove the green mask. He said that he had deliberately left a small piece of green near her right ear so that he could be reminded of her escapade.

'You beast, you didn't tell me!' accused Chelsea, 'You mean to tell me that you let me walk around the main street of Surfer's with green gunk on my face?'

Jack raised his hands in defeat. 'Sorry, but it really was priceless, Chels. I always expected to arrive on a white steed and rescue a damsel from a dragon, not from green slime and an automated massage chair.'

Andrew talked about his latest client who managed the spa facility at The Marriot Resort. He handed Chelsea a voucher for a pamper pack at the spa. 'Perks of the job,' he said with a smirk. 'That will show you what real pampering is.'

Chelsea thanked him and Jade took Jemima to bed after many lingering good-byes and hugs to everyone. Jade returned half an hour later professing that Jemima made her more tired than a full day at the office.

'So like her mother,' laughed Andrew, pulling his wife onto his lap where she lovingly played with his hair. Chelsea was touched to see the obvious affection between the two. They had been married for sixteen years and still enjoyed each other. They were both energetic business people but Chelsea guessed that Andrew was the more restful. He was very relaxed. He obviously knew how to put aside the pressures of his real estate business and enjoy his family. Perhaps the fact that he was ten years older than Jade gave him the mature tolerance that he wore so well. He clearly adored her and she him.

When the evening shadows lengthened they all went indoors. The two men went into the kitchen to load the dishwasher, leaving the two women to chat over their mulled wine in the living room. Although Jade was extroverted and flamboyant the furnishings were subdued and elegant. The lounge chairs were soft kid leather in a subtle muted taupe and they were even more comfortable than the cane lounges at the beach house.

Chelsea noticed a photograph of an older man and woman on the sideboard. The man looked like Jack. It must be his father but the woman didn't match Jack's description of his mother so she assumed that this was the woman that his father had married, the country vet. Their heads were inclined towards each other and they looked the picture of mature love as they smiled into each other's eyes.

'That's our father and his new wife, Elise. It was taken at Emily's wedding last year.'

'They look very happy,' commented Chelsea.

'They are; he seems like a different man with her. It has taken me a long time to get my head around it but I can see now that dad is happier than he ever was with mum.'

'My father left us when I was twelve, but he was away so much that none of us really noticed the breakup, well, except for Alicia.

She was sensitive about everything. She is still angry and dad has been dead for years now.'

'I was twenty five and had been married over a year. I think Kylie took it the hardest, she was the only one of us still at home and she idolizes dad. She was devastated when he left. She was angry for a lot of years but she never cut ties with him, at least she visited him and worked her way through it,' Jade explained.

'Alicia was angry at dad for breaking the family up but I think that I had already stopped trusting him long before he left. He was always promising that we would stay in one place, that we would have family holidays and then he would come home and announce some new scheme or job that meant we only had days to pack up, say our goodbyes and leave.'

'That must have been so unsettling for you all. At least we were all adults when dad left. It was hardest for Kylie because mum became quite bitter for a while. We had never really seen mum angry before and she was enraged for a good twelve months. She was never really the same but at least she made friends with dad in the end before she died.'

'I think it would have been healthier if mum had been angry but she swallowed all her emotions. I used to think of her as the perennial victim; she always seemed so defeated. Whatever dad said, went. Not that he was ever harsh or controlling in an angry way. He was just full of dreams and schemes.' Chelsea drank the last of her wine.

'I guess I came to realise that they were only human,' said Jade. 'Would you like more wine?'

'No, thanks, I'm fine,' responded Chelsea. 'Jack doesn't talk about his father much, but I gather he wanted to be a lawyer like him.'

'Yes, when dad left he took Jack's dreams with him. Jack had always planned to come back and join the law firm that dad was partner in but when dad left he sold his share of the business. I don't think Jack and dad have ever talked about it, typical male reluctance. Each waiting for the other.'

'I know getting anything out of my brothers is like opening a clam.'

Jade leant forward and looked deep into Chelsea's eyes.

'So, what do you think of my brother? He's very taken with you, I can tell.'

'At first I thought he was an arrogant stuffed shirt.'

Jade laughed, 'What makes you think you got the arrogant part wrong!. Her voice had a teasing quality.

'I've seen another side to him. I love his sense of humour—it was so unexpected, so playful. He's not as stiff and serious as I thought. At first I just wanted to shake him.'

'Oh I think you have done that alright. You're good for him; real and natural. You're not his usual type of woman.'

'I'm not?'

'No, but that's a good thing. He usually has cold pretentious models on his arm.'

'Then I am really not his usual type,' said Chelsea, pleased to get this insight from Jack's sister.

'You're a breath of fresh air—he comes to life around you. I've never seen him enjoy anyone so much. He is usually parallel to the woman in his life but with you he is connected. One thing is for sure, you'll never bore him.'

The clinking noises in the kitchen had stopped and the men joined them. It was getting late and Jade and Andrew had enough on their plate with Jamie in hospital so she rose and thanked them. Jack's eyes met hers with grateful understanding.

Jack and Chelsea sat in the sunroom of the beach house nursing steaming hot chocolates. Chelsea had made Leisa's special recipe that contained chilli and topped it with whipped cream. The sliding door was open to let the subtle sea breeze in. Chelsea was leaning into Jack with her head resting on his shoulder. She felt like she had known him forever. His arm was casually draped around her.

'Your father looks happy in the photo, the one in Jade's living room,' she said, a little afraid she might be intruding on his private pain but he had already shared so much of his life story with her.

'Yes, I really think he is,' Jack said putting his mug on the glass coffee table and drawing her close, 'It's funny, when you're young you don't think of your parents as happy or unhappy. I never thought they were miserable, but I guess they must have been or they would have stayed together.'

'I know what you mean; my parents were so fastidious about never arguing in front of us. Which was a noble principle but it meant that we never understood when dad left. Not that any child can understand that I suppose.'

'I think dad always had a hankering for the simple things in life and when we were all through high school he saw no reason to stay.'

'I think my father just went where the wind blew him, I don't think he ever made a conscious decision in his life.' Chelsea turned to face him and he planted a soft kiss on her lips.

'It must be hard for you to have virtually lost both of them, your father to death and your mother to dementia.'

'It wasn't so bad when she remembered us, but now....' Chelsea wiped a tear and Jack bent down to kiss where the tear had fallen. 'We are familiar to her, but not as her children, she greets us as old acquaintance, but if tell her we are her daughters or sons she becomes quite agitated and says, 'I've never had children, what are you saying?' so of course we just accept how things are.'

'The mind is a marvellous thing.'

'The experts have a simple rule, the last information in is the first out, so while she can be very clear about pets she had in childhood she won't remember where her room is. Alicia is very angry and predictably blames dad.'

'But you?' Jack questioned.

'Who knows, she had enough stress in her life. But she seems less worried somehow; it's hard to put my finger on it. I guess her mind has just chosen a softer reality in her past. She seems like someone I don't know and yet so dear and familiar. It was hard because she was so young when we found out, she was only 49.' Chelsea sighed.

'That is young, how did she take it?'

'Like everything else, she just resigned herself to it. That made me angry I wanted her to fight, but giving in was a lifetime habit I guess.'

'You must miss her.'

'I miss who she was, the woman who waltzed around the kitchen with us and let us build indoor cubbies on rainy days. Do you miss your mother?'

'More than I thought I would actually. She was larger than life, Jade is so much like her, so is Emily, Kylie is more like dad. Mum would fill the room. I think she overshadowed dad a little.'

'Did that worry him?'

'He actually seemed to like that she took centre stage. It took the pressure of him. He was never fond of socializing; he sometimes said she lived in a false world. After his partner in the law firm committed suicide he changed. Mum tried to bring him out of it but he just got worse. And then he left. I got one phone call from him, and a barrage of calls from mum. It was as if he just let her have centre stage completely.'

'So you have never talked about any of this with him?'

'There didn't seem much point. What could I gain from rehashing the past?'

'Oh I don't know, understanding, clarity, you know that sort of thing. I regret that I didn't talk frankly to mum. And now it's too late.'

'Men just get on with things. Men don't do that,' Jack murmured as he bent to kiss her.

'What do men do then, Stretch?'

'I'm glad you asked Scheherazade, I'm glad you asked.' He began a slow sensual assault that had become familiar and erased every reasonable thought out of her mind.

Chapter 11

'I cannot believe I am here in the middle of a reptile park. Whatever possessed the writers to set the scene in this God forsaken place? This new ratings 'push' is pushing my buttons.' Gavin was loudly complaining as Emma was giggling and trying to apply his make-up. Chelsea was glad to see the two of them had reconciled their differences and were back to being friends again. Emma winked over Gavin's shoulder at Chelsea.

'I know they want to increase the ratings but why would the urbane Blair Chase take his son to a reptile park and lose him there. What are the writers thinking?' Gavin was obviously way out of his comfort zone, preferring the glamour of the city sets. 'Not that I mind the outdoors, in small doses that is, but crocs and snakes aren't my thing.' The constant changes to the script had all the cast on edge.

'Gazza, sit still for goodness sake, I can't put makeup on when you talk,' remonstrated Emma brandishing a cosmetic brush.

'It isn't going to stay on long in this heat anyway,' complained Gavin. 'Where is my 'son' anyway? Has anyone seen Turbo?' Gavin was referring to his on-screen son Jackson, who was played by Josh Brandon.

'You can't believe how thrilled Sophie our producer was when she discovered that you were a qualified pre-school teacher Chels, she positively purred when she found out. They would've had to delay the filming because they have to have qualified staff and the usual teacher has called in sick.' That explained the eagerness of the producer to have Chelsea on set today. Emma threw down the brush in disgust and told Gavin that he would have to make do as she'd had enough of him for one day.

'As long as I have my sunscreen I will be fine m'dear,' he said giving Emma a placating hug. 'There you are Turbo, come here to daddy, or you will end up as croc bait.' Gavin reached for the wriggling eight year old and threw him squealing over his shoulder. 'Where's your mum?' Turbo pointed at Susan Ells who played his screen mother. She was being attended to by Emma.

'Your real mother, you confused brat!' corrected Gavin, bouncing Turbo on his knee. 'Where is Sandra?'

'I don't know, Uncle Gaz, maybe she's in the snake pit.'

'You're too cheeky for your own good, kid,' said Gavin turning him upside down making him shriek with laughter. 'I'll give you the snake pit!'

'No, no, no! Not the snake pit, Uncle Gaz!' squealed Turbo.

'Over-actor,' said Jack depositing him on the nearest deck chair.

'That's what I pay him for,' said Sophie, the producer as she approached with Jade, Jack and Jemima. Jemima was going to be an extra again and Jack and Chelsea had her for the day while Jade visited Jamie in the hospital.

'Where are your leg braces?' said Jemima to Turbo.

'I don't really need braces silly, that is just a part I play as

Jackson,' said Turbo eyeing the newcomer with caution. 'What's your name?'

'Jem, I'm an extra today. I have to faint when they milk the spiders.'

'Cool. I bet you faint anyway. Girls hate that stuff.'

Sophie turned to Chelsea and explained. 'We are required to have a qualified teacher on site for the children for Occupational Health and Safety regulations but because it is the holiday it is just a formality really. Are you OK with that?'

Chelsea thought it was a bit late in the day for that request but nodded in agreement. Sophie thrust a clipboard towards Chelsea and asked her to sign. She looked at Jack and he gave a small nod of approval. She signed where Sophie's red nail was pointing. It seemed like this was a working holiday after all. 'No such thing as a free lunch' she could remember her mother saying. It seemed that this was true.

'I hate this outdoor stuff,' moaned Sophie as she adjusted her straw hat. She seemed to relax now that the paper work was done. 'Let's get this show on the road.'

The morning passed quickly and Chelsea was surprised once more at the business like professionalism of the cast. Even Gavin forgot his complaining and instantly became the brooding bitter music producer, Blair Chase. Today's filming centred around Blair taking his son Jackson, from his previous marriage on an access visit to the reptile park.

At least Chelsea knew a bit more about the soap after watching the DVD's with Jack. Even though they had done more chatting and kissing as they dipped fruit into the chocolate sauce they had bought at the deli. Chelsea knew that Blair, the main character had been married three times even though he was only in his mid-thirties. Jackson, played by Josh Carter (aka Turbo), was his son by Belinda his second wife. Blair was embroiled in a bitter custody battle with Belinda over Jackson. Blair had married Brittany, an up and coming rock singer, and she was a brittle ambitious woman who had married Blair for his wealth and lifestyle as a music producer.

Because of the slump in ratings the show's writers were continually pushing the envelope with the story lines and many of the actors were not happy. Susan Ells who played Brittany commuted from Melbourne where she lived with her actor boyfriend who was currently working in the theatre. Rumour had it that she was looking for other opportunities because she wasn't thrilled with her role as a vacuous trophy wife. There was even talk that she wanted to further her singing career. Chelsea soon found that Susan was the consummate professional and while the others joked or complained she just got on with things.

Blair, Brittany and Jackson were filmed walking around the various attractions at the reptile park. There was a mysterious rough stranger lurking in the park watching the two of them and waiting to snatch Jackson. Jackson mysteriously disappeared; 'kidnapped' by his mother Belinda and her offside to cause trouble for Blair and his new wife.

Belinda's henchman snatched Jackson while Blair and Brittany were arguing over Blair's long hours at the music studio and on the road with his various music artists. Brittany accused Blair of losing interest in her. Brittany collapsed in hysterical grief in Blair's arms just as Jackson was being loaded unconscious into a van with darkened windows where his mother Belinda was waiting.

As usual there were more technicians than actors. While the other actors were filming Jack and Chelsea wandered around the vast complex with Jemima and Turbo and his mother Sandra. In the manner of all children Turbo and Jemima became instant friends with the usual mix of curiosity and bluntness.

'You're quite big for five,' said Jemima.

'I'm not actually five silly, I'm really eight and a quarter years old,' responded Turbo, drawing himself up to his full height. 'Television shows get older kids to play parts so they look smarter.'

'Oh, I see,' said Jemima who didn't appear to see at all. 'Well I guess I must really be four then.'

'You're just an extra, so it doesn't matter,' said Turbo pleased to be older and wiser.

Jemima had really enjoyed being an extra in Le Cirque but was getting very weary of the whole process as the day wore on. Thankfully the scenes involving the children were done just before lunch because of the regulations for child actors. Jemima fainted beautifully several times and was quite cross by the fourth time.

'I don't like snakes, they're ugly and ridiculous,' she said.

'You should see the Noctarium,' suggested Turbo, 'they have the coolest possums and sugar gliders there.' Turbo was usually the youngest on set and often the only child so he was delighted to have company of his own age.

'Oh wow,' trilled Jemima, instantly recovered and pulling on Jack's arm, 'can we go see Uncle Jack, please, *please!*'

Chelsea, Jack and Sandra were joined by Emma and Gavin who professed a great desire to see possums in all their nocturnal glory. Gavin threw a delighted Turbo over his shoulder. Jemima followed carrying a long stick.

'Don't run with that stick, Jem,' cautioned Jack.

'I'm dragging it, Uncle Jack,' said Jemima, trailing the stick behind her. Chelsea held Jemima's hand and walked beside Gavin. Jack was talking to Sandra and Emma and Chelsea stole sideways glances, admiring his gentle grace and warm humour. She wondered how she had ever thought him dull as she watched his keen intense eyes. She loved the way he relaxed into life. He was so comfortable with himself, so self-assured. She realised that she had mistaken arrogance for confidence. She loved his calm determination. She stopped her wayward thoughts, when had the word 'love' popped into her mind. Focusing on the children she went and stood beside them.

'That's Fat Albert,' said Turbo, pointing to a pair of gleaming black eyes. 'He is the biggest possum in the world and he has lived here forever.' Turbo leaned back with the air of one who had just truly earned expert status.

'Where?' said Jemima, 'I can't see a possum.'

'There, silly,' said Turbo, grabbing her stick and pointing in the direction of the gleaming eyes.

There was a scream from Jemima as Fat Albert ran up the stick, over Turbo shoulders, up Chelsea's arm and scuttled into the bush.

'Now, you've done it, you silly girl!' yelled Turbo.

Jemima burst into tears. 'You put the stick in there, you stupid boy,' she howled.

Jack and Sandra rounded the corner in the Noctarium. Chelsea wrapped her arms around Jemima and explained what happened to the others.

'I'm in big trouble aren't I Uncle Jack, we let the possum out, the reptile park people will be really cross, they will have a big search, they will want me to pay, I don't have any money Uncle Jack,' Jemima burst out.

Jack bent down and placed his hands on her shoulders. Very quietly he said, 'It is OK sweetheart, no one is going to be in trouble. Possums live in the bush, it is their natural home and possums are not dangerous, there won't be a search or anything else. Okay?'

Jemima sniffled. Turbo patted her on the head happy now that there was no need to blame anyone. Jemima shot him a poisonous glare.

'We don't even need to say anything about it,' added Jack. 'I think it is about time we went home, don't you Chels?'

'Oh, yes please,' responded Chelsea, 'if I see another scaly creature or a camera for that matter I will scream.'

Jemima walked between them maintaining her sulky air of indifference. Sophie met them in the car park and Chelsea was surprised to hear that they would all be paid the going rate as extras. Chelsea shot Jack a curious look but he stilled her with his eyes. She wouldn't mind betting that Jack had something to do with that decision even though Sophie was acting as if she had merely omitted to mention it before.

'You don't have to come in tomorrow Chelsea,' said Sophie, 'It is your last full day here. There are probably things you would rather do. There are lots of great boat tours on the Broadwater canals, so many fabulous homes of the rich and famous to see. I can get you vouchers if you like.'

Chelsea spluttered. She had seen about as much as she could take of wealth and fame. She politely declined and was pleased to see a grateful smile on Jack's face.

'Meet up with us at Le Cirque tomorrow night m'dears,' said Gavin. 'We will have some goodbye drinks.' He looked down at Emma who had her arm looped casually through his. Emma mouthed a thank you to Chelsea. Chelsea smiled back in recognition.

'We'll see you then,' said Jack.

Jemima was sound asleep five minutes into the drive home with her arms wrapped around the huge green inflatable toy crocodile that Jack had bought her. Jack put a CD on and the sultry sounds of the singer relaxed Chelsea. Jack drove with the same calm focus that he did everything. Chelsea had never enjoyed car travel, probably because there were four children in the family and the only memories she had of travel were of long tense journeys where constant arguments erupted between the children about who was invading someone else's space.

She remembered her mother's fruitless attempts to maintain peace and her father's erratic driving. He drove the way he lived, with one eye on the job and the other on anything else that moved. Jeff had been an angry driver, his flamboyant good humour evaporating in the first few minutes as he swore at everyone on the road. Driving with Jack was pleasant indeed and Chelsea drifted off.

Chelsea couldn't believe what she was reading. She had just stopped in at the studio to collect some of her things and had found a script in the staffroom. It was to replace the scene she had written. It had the same elements but it was so different in intention that she was appalled. She was so angry that she had stuffed it into her purse, called a taxi and left.

She couldn't believe that this was happening after she had already been present for the filming of the original scene. She had heard about this sort of thing happening; about actors having their whole involvement in a movie cut on the editing room floor. She wouldn't have minded that but she found the replacement scene abhorrent.

Jack had taken Jemima home and had arranged to meet her back at the beach house later. She sat in the sunroom fuming. How dare they? This was a twist that she hadn't expected. She cursed herself for not being prepared. Of course, they would use her writing and give it their own interpretation. She should have known this could happen. She was tired and she needed a friend. She needed Jack.

The fact that she was cursing herself for ever feeling like needing a man only added to her disquiet. Her phone call to Leisa had only heightened her unease because Leisa's only advice had been to lean on Jack. After all, he was a lawyer. Chelsea's protestations that he was connected to the show only made Leisa more adamant that Chelsea waste no time in telling him.

Chelsea fretted and paced, willing the clock to slow down and

Jack to hurry. By six in the evening she had stewed for two hours and even a short swim in the pool had not cooled her nerves. She was trying to distance herself from the problem. Her mother had always said that she needed to sleep on every problem because she was impulsive and everything would look clearer in the morning. This had been a valuable lesson for Chelsea as a child but how she chafed.

Torn between a desire to sort things immediately and also keep a cool head she was relieved when Jack's car pulled in. Chelsea retreated to the sunroom, suddenly shy of Jack. They had been lovers for the past few days but she was feeling a chasm between them and she hadn't even talked to him yet. Their relationship had been playful and relaxed. How would they deal with reality showing its ugly face? She hesitated to bring problems into their budding relationship, but she had no choice, she was hopeless at pretending everything was fine.

Jack found her in the sunroom with her arms wrapped around her knees, folded into the love seat. He knew at a glance that something was wrong. His heart sank. He had tried so hard to get close to this wonderful woman and he sensed a breach. His fists knotted. He would take on whoever had caused this sadness. He looked at her worry lined face as she met his gaze with clear honest eyes.

'Spill,' he said.

The story came out in a tumble of words. She said how she had come across the script and handed it to him to read. Although the key elements were the same Jack could instantly see that the interpretation was so far removed from what Chelsea had written to make it almost unrecognisable.

Where the electric blanket had been put on high by Brittany as a prank on an indifferent Blair to tease him about wanting his bed hot, this had been turned into a malicious attempt on his life.

Likewise the accidental adding of disinfectant to his candlelight dinner had been turned into an attempted poisoning. In the final part of Chelsea's written 'scene' where Brittany was supposed to set fire to Blair's newspaper to get his attention this had been turned into a vicious attack where Blair was close to death in an induced coma in hospital with severe burns to his body.

Jack felt Chelsea's outrage. He sat in the chair opposite and began to talk her through things in his calm deliberate manner.

'You signed a contract to allow them to do this Chelsea,' he said.

Her eyes were instant lasers, bright and indignant. 'So there is nothing I can do about this, this outrageous nonsense.'

'I didn't say that, I'm being devil's advocate here.'

'Well, I was hoping that you would be *my* advocate, I was stupid to even tell you. You are their legal representative, not mine. They are the ones paying you. I have nothing more to say to you. I can't afford you.'

And with that she ran out the sliding door, wrapping her shawl around her. Jack ran frustrated fingers through his dark hair. He was not going to chase her down the beach when she hadn't let him say more than a few words. He would wait until she cooled down and then he would approach things again.

Chelsea's mind was churning. She heard her mother's words so oft repeated in her childhood. 'You can't always run away Chelsea, you are running from yourself.' She hesitated, and then turning back she saw Jack watching her, patiently and quietly.

She slid back into the room, this time choosing the stool near the door. She crossed her arms; poised for flight.

'Alright, I'm listening, but I can't afford your hourly rate.'

Jack ignored her hostility and calmly went on.

'I don't work for the television studio, I don't work for Jade's PR firm, and I don't work for the advertising agency that promoted the prize or the soap opera.'

Chelsea's eyes filled with confusion.

'I don't understand,' she said.

'My only involvement with this was to step in for Jade to present the prize. She had planned to travel to Sydney but Jamie had to be taken for emergency surgery the afternoon she had planned to fly out and she rang me to fill in for her.'

Chelsea's mind threatened to go blank.

'Well, what are you doing here this week?' she questioned, now diverted from her original thought pattern. Her voice had come out as an alarming warble that was at least one octave higher than she planned.

Jack ran his hand through the short black curls on his forehead. He was hoping to avoid this conversation. 'I'm on holiday,' he said, praying she would accept that explanation. Not a chance, her eyes flared.

'Really,' Chelsea said, and was then disgusted that her voice went even higher if that were possible. 'How, how ... convenient.'

Jack struggled under her pointed gaze. He would rather have dealt with the problem at hand and was greatly unsettled that he had to introduce his deception now. He was hoping to tell her later when they had time to get to know each other better and they could laugh about it. But the look in Chelsea's eyes told him she was far from laughing.

'Look, can't you just let me deal with this first,' he said waving the script towards her.

'And what convenient plot have you cooked up in this convenient life of yours to deal with that. Do tell, counsellor.' There was a dangerous gleam in her eyes and Jack felt a flush creep over his face. Any other woman would be flattered at the hint that he had changed his holiday plans to get to know her, but Chelsea wasn't any other woman.

Jack cleared his throat. His role as protector was in jeopardy here and he forced himself to return to the subject. He would talk about his presence in Surfer's later.

'The way I see it you can't refuse outright to let them do the script their way, however we can try to apply pressure for them to do it. Failing that I may be able to persuade them to take your name out of the advertising. They have broken the original contract by changing the prize details by altering the venue and the reality television aspect. I will remind them of that and say that you will waiver all entitlements if they rewrite it. That should give us some leverage. You can trust me on this, I will work it out.'

Just the mention of the word trust touched her but she refused to show it.

'Can I come with you?'

'No, it will be more professional if I go alone.'

'So you will fix this for me, just like that?' said Chelsea, stunned.

'I think I can negotiate our way out of this,' he affirmed.

The torrent of words that Chelsea had running through her mind for the last few hours shrank and then faded in her mind. He had said 'our'.

'And I should just trust you and let you do this?'

'Yes,' he said, his eyes pleading for her to understand. She looked into his calm confident eyes and found a new emotion forming for this man, respect. All the careful arguments that she had rehearsed in the last two hours to combat the problem just dissolved. She tried to recall them but failed.

'And what will your fee be for this service, counsellor?' she said, a smile beginning to play on her lips.

'As you so ably put it Scheherazade, you can't afford me.'

Chapter 12

Jack leant on the doorjamb of the secretary's small office on the 47th floor of Maitland Towers. This was where the executives of the television station Channel 4 had their offices. They were responsible for 'Daydream Island'.

Jack had phoned Jade the previous night and she had given him the private number for Malcolm Yates who was the executive responsible for the soap opera. Jack had contacted him at home that night as soon as Chelsea had talked to him about the scene.

Malcolm had been calm and offhanded but many years of dealing with people had given Jack a unique awareness of the undercurrents of human interaction. He sensed that there was an underlying tenseness in the man. When he had informed Malcolm that he was the lawyer representing Chelsea Prentiss the man had been curious and worried but had struggled to hide both emotions.

Jack knew that the television executives had been very anxious about the negative publicity that they would endure if this widely advertised prize backfired on them. He knew that more than the reputation of the soap opera was at stake. The television station itself would bear the brunt of any unfulfilled promises.

Malcolm had gruffly requested the purpose of the phone call but Jack had wisely told him that he wished to see him in person and negotiate when he could present all the facts. Malcolm had then made an appointment at his office for nine o'clock the following morning but rather tersely informed Jack that he didn't have much time.

Jack had gained the distinct impression that the soap opera was under a cloud and it was widely known that the ratings had fallen seriously when the main character Blair had suffered from a mysterious case of amnesia. Many of the critics had begun to pan the soap saying that it had pushed the envelope too far into non reality and wouldn't last. Jack hoped to play this card in his favour.

While he was waiting for his appointment Susan Ells had arrived to collect her pay from Janice the receptionist for Malcolm Yates. Susan smiled warmly at Jack and asked if he had recovered from the day with the reptiles. Janice was agitated and she was unaware that Jack had an appointment with Malcolm.

Malcolm arrived abruptly and took Jack straight into his office. He was all urban charm and offered Jack a chair. He was a tall and charismatic man who had hosted several game shows before taking on his present role.

'I won't play games Jack. I am a straight shooter. There are moves afoot for 'Daydream Island'. I am not at liberty to discuss them at present but I do want to reassure you that we regret any inconvenience that Ms Prentiss has experienced due to the changes to her prize and are prepared to negotiate for her satisfaction. Daydream Island isn't our only concern at the television station and I am sure you are cognizant of the fact that we wish to avoid a publicity nightmare. Ms Prentiss has been most obliging and we wish to accommodate her. That said; we are not prepared to offer any monetary amount other than the wages she would receive as an extra for the filming. I have a cheque her for a further $5,000 to that effect, should Ms Prentiss be amenable.'

Jack leant back into the soft leather chair and hid the enormous relief that he was experiencing. His bluff on the phone last night had paid off. They were prepared to listen.

'Ms Prentiss is deeply concerned that having already been involved in writing a scene for the show and seeing that scene filmed it has now been scrapped. She is even more distressed that it is to be replaced with a scene that has been adapted from her writing but which she feels destroys her creative process. She wishes to withdraw her name and protect her authorship and thus her reputation, from this new interpretation.'

It was Malcolm Yates' turn to be relieved and hide that relief. Jack saw his hand relax the grip on his pen; a good poker player would now know who held the winning hand. And Jack knew he had won.

'I feel confident that I can give you my solemn and complete undertaking that her wishes will be carried out. I will invite my secretary in now and have that in writing and signed for you, if you would care to wait for a few minutes.'

Wrapped in Jack's arms in the emerald grotto that was The Natural Arch Chelsea thought about the past week. It had truly been a week in paradise. The sounds of the waterfall that filled the cavern were elemental and peaceful and from their perch high on the huge rock in the centre of the underground pool it felt as though they were the only two people on earth. Chelsea nestled closer to Jack. The soft mist of the cool water caressed their skin. The Natural Arch was a huge underground cave that was like nature's indoor pool. The waterfall fed the deep green pool and the sunlight entered with the waterfall giving it a magic appearance.

They had been swimming for the last half hour and now they reclined on the smooth black rock.

Jack had certainly kept his promise to her. Early that morning she had found him in the kitchen with his briefcase, a piece of toast and a mug of coffee. The night before he had stilled her doubts with his lips and his body. The unease that returned when she awoke was dispelled at the sight of Jack ready to do battle for her. She had realised then that she could handle defeat because even if they were to fail they were on the same side.

But Jack had come back to the beach house with the optimistic news that the television executives had accepted Jack's proposal, the replacement scene would be dropped. Chelsea had not only been relieved by the news but she had been thrilled that her faith in Jack had been so beautifully rewarded.

After he had left to go to the studio and speak with the television executives she had cried hot tears of frustration and had admitted to herself that she was tied to feelings that were embedded in her past experiences. Her father's abandonment had left her vulnerable and afraid to trust. She had fought her own battles and made her own way through university and life. She had partied with friends and denied that the past affected her.

But now she was out of her depth with her feelings for Jack she realised that for the first time in her life she had relinquished a problem and entrusted it to another person. It had been a huge struggle to let Jack step in and she was in a turmoil wondering if he would come through for her or be like her father with his endless broken promises.

She realised that her feelings for Jeff, her former boyfriend, had been shallow. They had never been tried and tested with reality. They had not faced any of the battles of life together. She had spent her time fitting in with Jeff and his life. She realised that her reluctance to have Jeff move in had been based on the subconscious knowledge that he would let her down. Something told her that Jack was different.

She pressed closer to him on the velvety rock and was rewarded by his strong arms embracing her. Chelsea had thanked him and apart from a simple, 'You're welcome' he hadn't brought the subject up again. Having two brothers had taught her that their approach to solving problems was very direct and she realised that for Jack the situation was over. She usually wanted to rehash and analyse everything but knew that his simple actions negated the need for that. It was one of the basic differences between men and women.

If Leisa had been here the two women would have whiled away a couple of hours looking at things from every possible angle. For the first time in her life Chelsea had just let it go, and it felt very good. She could get used to this.

'I could stay here forever,' she whispered into Jack's ear, sending fire through his veins.

'You have certainly taken to the water like a mermaid. I must be a very good teacher,' said Jack smugly.

'Trust you to take the credit,' she said with a laugh. 'But I think your techniques would get you into hot water with the Board of Swimming Studies. They would revoke your license.'

'Or pay me double,' he said nibbling her neck.

'Tell me a story, my Scheherazade.'

Chelsea turned to face him and thought for a moment.

'There was a Sultan who was a just and kind ruler. His wife however, proved false. He became so angry at her betrayal that he had her beheaded.'

'That is one bitter man,' muttered Jack.

'Don't interrupt the soothsayer. The Sultan determined that he would never be played for a fool again. But he loved women so he decided that he would take a new bride every day and have her executed the following day. That way no other woman would ever have a hold on him and destroy his trust.'

'These are brutal. I hope they weren't children's bedtime stories. There would have been a whole nation of weeping and wailing.'

'They are adults' stories. They came from before the time of the written word. And you are partly right; there was indeed a whole nation of weeping and wailing. Mothers and fathers weeping for the daughters who were brides for one day only and then slain by the bitter Sultan. Finally a young woman of great wisdom and insight offered herself as his bride. She begged him to hear her tales and ask to be granted one more night of life to tell him stories.'

'Good grief,' said Jack and was hushed immediately by Chelsea.

'She was truly wise and told him tales of high adventure, of heroes and villains, of greed and valour.'

'Smart girl, no chick stuff.'

'Of course, while she had tales to tell she lived. And as she had planned, the Sultan fell deeply in love with her, thus sparing the lives of many maidens. They went on to have many children but sadly only one son, the Caliph prince Jakistani. The Sultan was a feared warrior and went on many holy crusades. One day he did not return.'

'I'm getting suspicious of this tale, Scheherazade.'

'The Caliph was pampered by his mother and his sisters and lived a life of ease. He ruled in his father's place and was fair and just and wise. But his every wish was carried out even before he thought it.'

'I don't like where this is going,' muttered Jack.

'Many women came to court to impress the Caliph but he had no need of any of them. He was after all, a spoilt brat. Ouch,' said Chelsea as Jack nibbled her ear.

'I can take it from here, Scheherazade. The Caliph was a fierce warrior like his father but he was well versed in the artistry of words and eschewed combat. He took the road of peace and justice.'

'Oh right!' muttered Chelsea.

'Although many fine women had tempted him with womanly wiles he was merely polite and gentle to them.'

'You're quite good with fiction.'

'Then one day he ventured into the tents where the maidservants cared for the children of the harem,' said Jack with a twinkle in his eye.

'Servants huh!'

'Do not interrupt the soothsayer. And there he found the most beautiful creature he had ever seen. With eyes of emerald, hair like nutmeg, lips like honey—sticky that is. Ouch... It was not permitted for him to be in the tents of the children of the harem but he was so bewitched by this stunning creature that he hid in a huge earthen vase so that he could hear her sing to the children and tell tales of bold adventure. He didn't let her see him because he was afraid she would run away.'

'Until the maidservant poured boiling oil in the vase,' laughed Chelsea.

'You're a heartless wench,' moaned Jack.

'I think you have missed your calling counsellor.'

They took a leisurely drive to Lamington National Park. On the way they saw an old limestone house that had been converted to a restaurant and they stopped for lunch. The restaurant was a series of rooms. The timber floorboards were polished and there was a huge fireplace in every room. Each of the rooms had wide open doorways between them. Linen tablecloths in mustard check adorned the tables.

The waiter was a middle aged man who was proud to tell them that he was also the owner and that he would personally cook their meal. Everything was home grown organically, he was proud to inform them and if they wanted fresh eggs he would go now and get them from the hen house. Chelsea was enchanted and said she would have a platter of vegetables with hand churned butter and two boiled eggs with Hollandaise sauce.

Jack was not suitably impressed with this choice and asked rather cheekily how long it would take to catch a cow. The maître d' took this in good spirit and gave a loud chuckle and said he would bring sir a steak. Sir was thrilled.

With the city so far away and the air so clear they both relaxed. This was their last night of the holiday week and Chelsea was glad they were flying back to Sydney together. The feeling that she had known Jack forever had increased with each day spent in his loving arms. She worried her bottom lip with her teeth as she thought of the days ahead and how they would fare back in the glare of their everyday lives.

'I don't think I want to go back to the city,' murmured Jack, reaching across to take her hand. Apparently he was thinking the same thing. 'This had been the best holiday ever, Scheherazade.'

'You read my mind, again. You have an alarming habit of doing that.'

'They say two people who have the same Karmic energy have that kind of connection,' he added.

'That is very 'sensitive new aged guy' of you,' observed Chelsea.

'No, it just comes from living in the Sultan's palace surrounded by women,' he teased.

'So you listened well, that's good. There will be a test later.'

'I can't wait,' said Jack with a sensual drawl. 'There won't be any boiling oil, will there?'

'No, but now that you mention it, I do have some massage oil that was as expensive as the original myrrh and frankincense.'

'Do you now? And where pray tell did you get that?' he asked, his grin spreading.

'At the day spa that Andrew gave me the voucher for. When I

told them I had autographed photos of Gavin they gave me a huge basket of samples in exchange for them.'

'Well, lucky you. But how did you manage to have a few hours of pampering and not need rescuing?'

'I had a choice of treatments and so I had a hot rock massage, a salt rub and a steaming soak in the hot tub. It was true bliss.'

'I am jealous. You weren't accosted by mutant chairs?'

'Not a one. I am now a convert. And I wish.'

'To share your good fortune with me.'

'Yes, I do.' Chelsea rested her hand on his thigh.

'Watch it Scheherazade, or I will have to break the speed limit to go home and feed another hunger altogether and make that poor man who is out chasing a cow for my lunch very cranky.'

Their meals arrived and they made the best of the lazy holiday spirit by making leisurely work of them.

'So shall I meet the marvellous Leisa and her adoring family when we go back? I am   dying to sample her cooking. If it is anything like that chilli hot chocolate you made me I will have to make her my official caterer,' said Jack, holding her eyes expectantly. It was the first mention of the future.

'If the way to a man's heart is through his stomach, then the way to Leisa's heart is through complementing her cooking.'

'Ah, the secret to success, thanks for the 'heads up' on that. I will be sure to lavish praise on her.'

'Not too much or Mike will knock you flat.'

'Oh yes, the hunky Mike of the huge thighs,' Jack laughed.

Jack leaned forward suddenly serious, 'I want some of your tomorrows you know. Can I come and hear you tell the children stories? Do you have a vase big enough for me to hide in?'

Chelsea laughed. It was a joyous sound. 'No, you can only come if you contribute in some way, we don't allow spectators.'

'I could recount the voyages of Jack Sparrow, Buccaneer and

Captain of the high seas.'

'Then I would never get them asleep at nap time.'

They ordered coffee and Chelsea opened up the subject of the replacement scene.

'It really meant a lot to me, what you did for me today. Even if you hadn't been able to convince them, it was terrific to have you on my team.'

'I can't promise that I will always agree with you but I will always be on your team. You are a remarkable, fascinating woman and I am so glad I met you, Chelsea Prentiss.'

'And I you, Jack Devon.'

The mood was far more sombre at Le Cirque that night. Chelsea and Jack had arrived back in Surfer's Paradise to the shocking news that 'Daydream Island' had been axed. It was a sharp contrast to the party atmosphere a few nights before when all the cast had posed for their portraits for the mural. Susan Ells had already booked her flight to Melbourne and she had come to Le Cirque to give moral support to Gavin and the others. She had been on the verge of resigning and was not personally devastated but she had come to regard the others as friends even though she hadn't socialised with them very much due to her frequent flights home to Melbourne.

She was pleased to have the time to invest in her rock band and push forward with her singing career. She had thought that the role as Brittany where she played a rock singer would have given her the opportunity to showcase her singing abilities but apart from a few minutes of air time singing she had spent her time acting the part of the spoiled diva and bitter wife.

'It's a relief really,' she said as Gavin handed her another colourful cocktail. 'The travel alone was killing me. My fiancé was always moaning.' Gavin pounced on the word fiancé and grabbed her hand.

'Wow, that is one gorgeous rock, my sweet, congratulations,' he purred, bestowing a gallant kiss on her cheek. 'Well, at least we have *some* good news to celebrate.' The cast gathered around and joined in congratulating her.

Jade and Andrew arrived with Jemima and shared the good news that Jamie was coming home from hospital in the morning. As Jade had been closely associated with the actors they were staying for dinner and Jemima climbed onto Jack's knee and chatted gaily to them all.

'This girl will be a real star one day,' Gavin said indicating Jemima.

'Don't say that, please,' moaned Andrew, 'she is enough of a drama queen now. After what we have been through with 'Daydream Island' I never want Jade to do public relations for a television show again. Unless it's a cooking show, of course.'

'Well, I am the only sad sack who is miserable tonight,' said Gavin.

'You're *always* a sad sack,' chimed Emma and Jade at the same time.

The younger cast members left with cheery and noisy good-byes and pronounced that they were off to do a round of the nightclubs and drown their sorrows.

'I have never seen a more cheerful bunch of people claiming the need to drown their sorrows, bah!' moaned Gavin.

'I am so going to miss you Gavin,' said Sophie laughing.

'It's alright for you Miss Producer, you probably have another show lined up already,' responded Gavin.

'Well, we are working on the pilot for a comedy series,' she teased.

'And of course you can't talk about it,' said Gavin.

'No, of course not,' said Sophie, 'apart from mentioning the fact that there may be a part for you Gavin.'

'Leave me alone unless you have something concrete,' he complained, 'I have been swinging like a pendulum for weeks now. What with all the changes and the new scenes, scrapping the old ones...*please*, I don't want to hear about anything. I think I will just pack up and go to Bali for a few weeks. Then I will check the Sydney scene out, I'm not returning to this God-forsaken part of the universe.'

'Speaking of returning, when we went back to the reptile park to film the aftermath of the kidnap scenes the staff of the reptile park were having a great time with one of the possums, Fat Albert, I think he's called.'

'Ooh Fat Albert,' squealed Jemima, 'that's the possum that we released to freedom, didn't we Chelsea?' Chelsea blushed and tried to give the seven year old a warning glance but knew the futility of trying to give seven year olds hints.

'Apparently he 'escapes' quite often and when he has had enough of the outside world he comes back and sits at the entrance waiting patiently for one of the animal wardens to put him back in the Noctarium,' explained Sophie.

'Daddy, I want a possum like Fat Albert,' begged Jemima.

'We brought you home a crocodile,' Jack interjected.

'Yes, but that was a plastic pet, I want a real pet. It could play with my imaginary friend Shannon and me.'

'I hope you don't mean a real crocodile Jem,' said Andrew.

'Don't be silly daddy, but I would like a real possum,' begged Jemima putting her bottom lip out and raising her hands in prayer in front of his face.

'Your brother is coming home from hospital tomorrow,' smiled Andrew, trying deftly to change the subject.

'He is worse than a crocodile,' pouted Jemima, then instantly brightening, 'Can we have a welcome home party? Please mummy?'

'Jamie won't be in the mood for parties Jem,' said an obviously weary Jade, 'but I guess we can put a few balloons up. But only if you come home now and go to bed early. We have to pick Jamie up first thing in the morning.'

Jemima was instantly off her chair and pulling her father's arm.

'Hurry up daddy,' she pleaded.

Andrew and Jade had taken that chance to say their goodbyes and that broke the friendly gathering up. Jack and Chelsea walked to Andrew's car with Jemima holding both their hands, swinging cheerfully.

Andrew and Jade both bid a warm farewell to Chelsea with Jade whispering in Chelsea's ear, 'Look after my brother, you're good for him.'

Andrew winked at Jack, 'If you have any sense, you'll keep her. Come back and see us soon—both of you.'

The engines of the 747 hummed. Chelsea had only flown several times in her life and she marvelled at the feeling of being thousands of feet in the air and yet feeling no different that if you were on a bus. She couldn't believe that the week was over and they would be back in Sydney in an hour.

'You're not going to nod off then?' she said to Jack who had her hand nestled in his.

'I was only pretending to sleep on the flight up to Surfer's,' Jack said, his eyes sparkling.

'Oh really, and what purpose did that serve, Stretch?'

'All the better to rest my head on your shoulder and drool over you.'

'I don't remember you doing that,' she said. 'Are you going to pretend to sleep this time?'

Jack's eyes roved her slim body. She was wearing khaki pants and a chocolate brown off the shoulder top. Her skin had acquired a golden glow. She looked delicious.

'Nope, I'm just going to drool.'

Chapter 13

Chelsea had one more week of her holiday time from the preschool and she moved into Leisa and Mike's home to help them with baby Hayden. Leisa and Mike's home was a large two storey house in Terry Hills and it was the base for Leisa's catering business. Bethany was holding the fort for the business but Leisa was anxious to be back on deck for the holiday round of catering events.

'Things will ease off in February, I only have three small corporate bookings,' said Leisa as she and Chelsea sat around the large table in the country style kitchen. Bethany was sitting with them and taking instructions for the Australia Day events that were booked. Leisa sat in the large rocking chair that Mike had made and gently rocked her newborn son.

'You and Mike should go away for a few weeks in February then,' remarked Chelsea. 'While you're here you will only get involved in the business and wear yourself out. Of course if you stopped being such a control freak and relax you'd be better off.'

'Don't you start,' muttered Leisa rubbing the back of her baby son, 'Charlotte has been at me to slow down.' Charlotte was Mike's mother who lived in their granny flat. She suffered from Multiple Sclerosis and was delighted to be a part of their daily lives. She adored her new grandson.

'How is Charlotte?' enquired Chelsea.

'She has good days and bad days. I have tried to tell her to take one of the downstairs rooms so we can keep a better eye on her but she won't hear a word of it. I would feel happier with her under our roof now that she is in a wheelchair most of the time.'

'She just hates being dependent,' added Bethany who was on her university break. She was studying for a degree in Social Science. Her mother Estelle was a nurse who came in twice a week to care for Charlotte. 'She is so thrilled to live with you and Mike; she doesn't want to be a burden.'

'She is going to need more care and even though Mike has installed a vital call system I still worry about her. The Rose Room at the back has a courtyard and a small sitting room. At least if she was there she could take advantage of the internal heating,' said Leisa.

'I think that if you approached it from the point of view that you need her, rather than basing the idea on her dependence then she might agree,' said Bethany wisely.

'I don't know how I would manage that,' said Leisa, intrigued. 'I have given her the bookwork to prepare for Richard our accountant, she is marvellous with that. I don't know what else I can do.'

'If you approached her and said you would love her to be able to watch over Hayden. Just say that it would be so handy to have someone in the house so that you can pop out for a few moments when he is asleep, I think that might work,' suggested Bethany.

'You're a genius Bethany,' said Chelsea, 'If you tell her that you have felt more secure with me here during this week and would like her to be under the same roof, she will feel useful and she loves Hayden.'

'That might just work,' said Leisa thoughtfully. 'You're brilliant Bethany; you will make a great social worker. Have you thought about what you will do after you graduate?'

Chelsea hid a smile. She knew that Leisa was desperate to have Bethany take on the role of full time manager of the catering business so that she could concentrate on the cooking side and have time with the baby.

'I am looking into working with the Western Region Health Service at the Women's Centre. I would like to get some real experience.'

'You're sure about that,' Leisa asked, 'I was hoping you would become my business manager, but if you are really keen to get in to social work then I will advertise for a manager. I am realising that looking after a baby takes a huge amount of time. And what has blown me away is that I am so in love with him, I just want to be with him all the time. Don't I darling?' she said tickling him under his wobbly chin.

'I will ask around the hospitality class at Uni if you like,' said Bethany.

'That would be good, thanks for that, the sooner I do something about it the better I will feel.' Leisa relaxed back in the rocking chair. Hayden was blissfully asleep, curved into her warmth.

'So then Chelsea,' said Bethany, turning to Chelsea with curious eyes, 'Tell me about this handsome lawyer of yours. I hear the original stuffed shirt turned into the handsome prince.'

Chelsea laughed, 'That about sums it up, I guess.'

'Oh come on Chels, you can do better than that, give us more than scraps here,' demanded Leisa, 'I haven't had time to catch up with you since you got back. So spill.'

'What changed your mind about him?' asked Bethany.

'Ladies, we have a social worker in our midst,' teased Chelsea.

'Give it up!' squealed Leisa, and then whispered as the baby stirred, 'Have a heart Chels.'

'Well, I disliked him on sight,' Chelsea began, 'I thought he was a pompous prat. He really got under my skin.'

'Sure sign of future attraction,' said Bethany. Chelsea shot her a poisonous look.

'He gave me such a rehearsed load of professional 'speak' that I wanted to slap him and ask him if he was a robot.'

'I bet you gave him *that* stare,' said Leisa, chipping in.

'What stare?' Chelsea gave Leisa an incredulous look.

'*Your* stare, it's a bit like that one,' she said pointing at Chelsea, 'but it is scarier, goes straight through you like a laser.'

'Must be the preschool teacher in her,' suggested Bethany helpfully, 'I'll bet the kids are too scared to lie to her.'

'You're worse than he is, the pair of you,' muttered Chelsea, 'I will tell you nothing if you keep side-tracking me too.'

'So *he* tries to side-track you does he? Poor Jack, I feel sorry for him,' added Leisa earning another sharp look from Chelsea. She zipped her mouth extravagantly and waited for Chelsea to continue.

'It was just the strangest thing, I have always known who I would be attracted to before and this has hit me sideways. I don't know if I am up or down. Sometimes he indulges me as if I am a child and other times he just sits and listens to me like one of my pre-schoolers.'

'He hangs off your every word. Ooh, that man is so into you,' cooed Leisa.

'Totally gone,' added Bethany.

'He is so different to any man I've known. I used to be attracted to the intense, controlling types who can lie at the drop of a hat. I was an 'arrogance junkie'. I thought calm nice men were boring; to tell the truth I thought he would be boring. It is the biggest surprise of my life so far.'

'What's so surprising? It's 'lurve',' said Leisa.

'It isn't so much Jack who has surprised you, it's your reaction to him,' said Bethany wisely.

'You know I think you're right.'

'When are you seeing him again?' asked Leisa.

'We're going sailing on the harbour tomorrow with his best friend Scott and his latest girlfriend.'

'Scott is his business partner too isn't he?' asked Leisa.

'Yes, he met him at Uni and they have been in business together since then. They go sailing all the time. I've never been. I hope I don't embarrass myself and spent the day throwing up over the side. That would be a great first impression!'

'Aha! First impressions are so fallible,' chortled Leisa.

'Aha yourself, smarty pants!' muttered Chelsea.

As it turned out Chelsea wasn't the one who spent the entire cruise bent over the rail of the 30 foot yacht. Tiffany, Scott's latest in a line of socialite girlfriends took that dubious honour. Chelsea was too tired to notice. She had been up all night with Hayden. She had given both Mike and Leisa the night off and they had gone to the restaurant in the Centrepoint Tower. Leisa had been eager to go there after Chelsea had said the food was to die for.

She had arrived on the wharf bleary eyed and exhausted. Scott and Jack had been there for an hour or so, getting the yacht ready to sail. Chelsea had phoned and said she would be late and Mike had dropped her off at the pier. Tiffany was all smiles and excitement. Chelsea wanted to knock her overboard. Jack had a bemused grin when Chelsea looked at Tiffany's animated spiel and she shook herself, afraid she might indeed by giving Tiffany 'the stare.'

Tiffany was condescending when she learned that Chelsea was a preschool teacher. Her superior airs grated on Chelsea but she bit her tongue. Jack seemed to find the whole situation highly amusing and this earned him 'the stare'. Oh dear, thought Chelsea, all I have to do is frown at Scott and the day will be complete.

'Mummy wanted me to go to Uni but my modelling agent suggested that I go to drama school. He said it would be a waste of talent not to go. So I took up acting,' Tiffany informed her gaily. She handed Chelsea a bottle of sunscreen.

'It's factor 30, we don't want wrinkles do we?' Chelsea thought knocking her overboard was too good for her. Jack's eyebrows appeared to be doing a little dance along with his expressive lips. He had never seen Chelsea tired and cranky and she was divine. It was better than any soap opera. He wondered when Chelsea would snap. He wasn't going to miss this for the world. Life before Chelsea had definitely been tame.

'You don't have a hat either, oh dear,' said Tiffany. Chelsea opened her mouth to respond but Tiffany was already on to the next subject, addressing Scott this time.

'There aren't any deck chairs. Where am I going to lie down and read?' she enquired. Jack turned away to hide his mirth.

'You don't have deck chairs on a sailing vessel, you only have them on cruisers,' Scott explained patiently. 'We'll have our time cut out trimming the sails and handling the yacht.'

This information did not seem to please Tiffany who had envisaged a day of idle pleasure. Scott was beginning to think that she was a lot less attractive today than when he had chatted her up at the recent charity event that he had attended. He was shocked to see that she was actually pouting.

'I didn't realise that sailing was so much work,' she said to Chelsea as they watched the two men expertly hoist the main sail and set about their work. Chelsea thought that if she bit her tongue once more it would be severed. Overcome with exhaustion she headed below deck and settled into one of the bunks. She was lulled by the gentle rolling of the yacht. It was like being in the rocking chair with Hayden and she fell asleep as soon as her head hit the pillow.

When she awoke she felt very much refreshed and ready to be human again, even to Tiffany. Pulling her caramel curls into a ponytail she jammed a blue and white striped cap on her head and pulled the ponytail through the opening at the back of the cap to secure it on her head. It was then she realised that the yacht was heaving and rolling in the waves.

She was surprised that she was enjoying the movement of the yacht and feeling invigorated she bounced up on deck to find a very subdued Tiffany grasping the rail on the side of the boat retching her heart out over the side. She actually felt sorry for the socialite.

She gave Jack a brief kiss on the neck as he was manning the huge steering wheel. His black hair was tousled by the wind. His sleeves were rolled up to reveal tanned, hard muscled forearms. He pulled Chelsea to him and encircled her in his arms. He yelled above the wind for her to try her hand on the steering wheel but she said she would check on Tiffany. Scott was hauling in the jib in order to decrease the sail area and slow the yacht down in the heavy seas. It was obvious that both men were in their element.

Tiffany was weakly clinging to the rail and her former pink healthy glow had been replaced with a greenish hue. She looked miserable as the yacht pitched up and down. Her hat had gone overboard and her towel was wrapped around part of the rail as it trailed in the water. Chelsea retrieved it and took her to the bow of the boat where she instructed Tiffany to look at the horizon. The boat was still pitching and rising but the roll was less noticeable there and Chelsea sat beside Tiffany.

Chelsea smiled and waved to Jack, thinking how dark and handsome he was and how he resembled his alter ego Jack Sparrow, the pirate Captain.

'You're damned cheerful,' muttered Tiffany when she had momentarily stopped retching.

Chelsea opened her mouth and shut it again. What was the use? Scott finished folding the jib he had hauled in and joined them. His solicitous enquiry of Tiffany's wellbeing only received a withering look and he shrugged and went to talk to Jack.

'I am never doing this again,' sputtered Tiffany, 'This is not my idea of a date, this is a nightmare. Scott better make this up to me, big time.'

Chelsea doubted that Scott had any plans to continue his relationship with Tiffany. From what Jack said his interest in any woman only lasted for a few dates anyway and Tiffany was giving every indication of being more high maintenance than a Hollywood starlet.

This was confirmed when they anchored. It had been calmer coming back to the quay and Tiffany had begun to pick up a little when the rolling had decreased. She even had her colour return a little until Scott said, 'Let's stop at the Fisherman's Co-op for a seafood basket. The girls can cook for us.'

Tiffany immediately headed for the rail again. Chelsea threw Scott a disdainful look and he gave a nonchalant shrug. He was certainly a cool customer thought Chelsea as she took in his youthful good looks. Blonde and well-built with a ready smile and a cheeky word he would have woman after him in droves. She couldn't believe she had thought Jack was spoilt. He looked like Mahatma Gandhi next to Scott.

When they reached the car park she saw Jack's sleek charcoal car.

'Do you mind if we drop Scott off? His car is at Geraldine's. Did

I tell you that Geraldine is Scott's grandmother? He is staying with her for a few days. You can meet her now if you like.'

'The old girl will love that,' said Scott as he gave an irate Tiffany a casual wave as she powered out of the car park in her red sports car. 'She can talk a torrent, and you can help me work my way through her pumpkin scones.'

It was a grand old house. From the stained glass door to the stone wall at the back of the yard Chelsea was enchanted. Not the least of all its marvels was Geraldine the owner. Jack had been right; they hit it off instantly.

The long hallway that went the length of the house had a formality that didn't prepare the visitor for the warmth of the interior. With highly polished timber floors throughout it had a liveliness of spirit. Built in the late 1950's by Geraldine's late husband Bert it had a unique character.

Geraldine was obviously very proud of the house. It was a real and lasting connection to her beloved Bert. They had been Ten Pound Poms; a part of the migration process of the post war period that promoted the immigration of over one million Britons to Australia. They were lured with the promise of a new life on the sundrenched relaxed shores of Australia.

Bert had been a lowly tradesman and he and Geraldine had married in spite of the opposition of her father who was a Barrister and the second son of an influential Earl. Geraldine's father had forbidden her to see Bert and she had not only defied her family to marry Bert but had followed him to a new life halfway around the world.

Chelsea learned all this in the first half hour that they were there. With her high cheek bones and gracious walk Geraldine was the quintessential upper class dame. She had an incredibly stylish short bob and her hair was elegantly white. One rheumy hand rested on her walking cane. Her mellow voice still had overtones of

England.

'I still miss England,' she said. 'I have loved two countries, but only one man.'

She loved her new country with a fierce loyalty. It had accepted her with the love of her life and given them a future when she had been disinherited by her family. After staying in a crowded hostel with other migrants where they had to take their own plug to the communal bathroom Bert had found work with a Sydney builder and hadn't looked back.

'It was easier for us because we didn't have children then. I felt sorry for those with children because they had such a time of it settling in. All we Poms assumed we would settle in immediately because we were from the Mother Country. It was quite a shock to be thought of as foreigners and job thieves. Some of our group went back but you had to pay the full fare back to the government. We couldn't have afforded that even if we had wanted to. It was ten pound each as long as we stayed for two years. Otherwise the fare was about one hundred and twenty pounds and very few could manage that amount of money.'

'I had never heard of that,' said Chelsea, intrigued. 'How marvellous.'

Jack rolled his eyes at Scott. 'Those scones will never see the light of day if we leave these two alone,' he muttered. Chelsea smiled. Jack was obviously at home here with Scott's grandmother.

'You just mind your manners young man,' reprimanded Geraldine. 'The pair of them nearly drove me mad when they stayed with me in their Uni days,' she grumbled.

Shooing them elaborately she set the table for their afternoon tea. Chelsea was immediately reminded of her own grandmother as Geraldine got a beautiful crystal butter dish from the fridge and another containing strawberry jam. Scott dipped his finger in the jam and received a swat on the back of his hand for his trouble.

'I thought you lived on campus when you were at Uni,' commented Chelsea confused.

'Oh we did, we just came here on and off to look after grandma,' Scott explained.

'What tosh,' exclaimed Geraldine. 'You came here to recover from lost loves and hangovers. I looked after you two. Talk about twisting the truth.'

'Chelsea is a freelance writer, Geraldine,' said Jack deftly changing the subject.

'How wonderful, what do you write dear?' she queried.

'Short stories so far,' said Chelsea. 'And I would like to write a novel one day.'

'She is very good,' Jack interjected, 'She wrote about your adventure with the con man.'

'Really! I would love to see that!' said Geraldine, leaning forward with great interest. 'You know, my son Eric, Scott's father is always telling me to write my memoirs; about the trip out here and starting our new life. We only had one suitcase between us, you know. Everything we owned was in one tattered case.'

'It must have been hard to leave everything behind,' said Chelsea.

'Oh my dear, you are wrong,' scolded Geraldine. 'I had everything with me; I had my Bert, you see.'

Over the next few months Chelsea called in to see Geraldine often. She began working on Geraldine's memoirs. Her writing was invigorated by the inspiration that Geraldine's life gave her. She suspected that it had also given Geraldine purpose. She certainly had a lively mind and even though she was in her nineties she was still very active.

Several months after their return from Surfer's Jack went to Hong Kong for ten days and Chelsea was shocked at how much she missed him. Their first week back had still had a relaxed feel as they were both still on holidays but the preschool had reopened a few days before Jack returned to work.

Chelsea was getting a taste of what it was like to be a part of Jack's very busy life. He worked six hectic days a week and often took work home. He loved to stay at Chelsea's flat in the northern suburbs. Chelsea realised why after the few times they had gone to Jack's inner city apartment. It was a luxury two bedroom townhouse but it was so devoid of personal items that Chelsea chided him that a ghost lived there.

It was all glass and muted greys. It resembled a work space and indeed that was what it was; a streamlined office. No wonder he could relax in her flat where there was a courtyard. Her second bedroom resembled the sunroom at the beach house and they spent many happy hours there.

While Jack was overseas Chelsea divided her spare time between visiting with Geraldine and Leisa and Mike's, enjoying her godson's growth. Leisa had employed a manager for the catering business. Amanda was a divorced woman who had previously managed her husband's Italian restaurant.

Amanda was a lively addition to the mix and it was her arrival that had solved the problem of encouraging Charlotte to move into the main house. When Leisa had asked Amanda when she could start Amanda had said she would be available as soon as she found somewhere to live. Charlotte had surprised Leisa by making the logical offer of the granny flat and so it was arranged. Amanda moved into the granny flat and Charlotte moved into the downstairs guest room. She was soon happy there and even seemed to be more energetic because with the ducted air conditioning she no longer had to suffer the oppressive heat of the granny flat.

When Jack returned he was clearly exhausted and for the first time he was also despondent. He seemed to have lost weight and when met him at the airport he told her that he had suffered from gastric flu while he was in Hong Kong. He arrived home on a Thursday and slept for most of the next two days. He was gratefully tucked up in Chelsea's flat.

'I'm sorry I have been such poor company,' he said when he surfaced Saturday morning to the smell of sausages and eggs. 'Wow that smells good.'

'I should hope so, Stretch. I was beginning to think you left your appetite in Hong Kong. But you haven't been poor company. Even asleep you were good company. At least you were here with me. I missed you.'

The enjoyed breakfast and coffee in the small courtyard and Chelsea was glad when Jack attacked his food with relish. After they went back inside Jack stacked the dishwasher and Chelsea cleared the food away. It was as if they had been a team forever.

'I hate the long hours away from you. I only saw you for a few hours at the weekend for the two weeks before I left. You owe me ten nights of stories, Scheherazade.'

Chelsea laughed.

'This story telling is getting to be a habit, Stretch. You're turning into the Sultan himself.'

'I love your stories.'

'No more Arabian Nights tales though, they are too gruesome by half,' she said as he lay across the lounge resting his dark head in her lap.

'No Arabian Nights then, just tell me about your days,' he said, reaching up to touch the sensitive part of her neck behind her ears. Her body buzzed as a current went down her spine leaving her nerves tingling.

'Duncan is coming two days a week now,' she began. Duncan was a delightful three year old who had cerebral palsy. Jack had met him when he visited Chelsea at the preschool and had the cute little guy giggling as he took him down the slippery dip time after time.

Jack had obviously spent a lot of time with his nieces and nephews Chelsea thought as he sang to Duncan, 'Up in the Air I Fly, zoom zoom, zooma zoom zoom'. Duncan couldn't talk or walk but as he sat lopsided in his pushchair, his mouth wide with delight he would clap his hands at the sight of Jack.

'Duncan is a cool little guy,' said Jack.

Chelsea told him about her other favourites. About the eighteen month old twins who were the youngest of ten children who hated to be apart, of how she worried that one of them was autistic because she always looked away and was behind all the others with her speech and movement. As she spun stories about her everyday life she stroked his forehead and was shocked to discover that he had fallen asleep again.

'I love you,' she whispered. Her hand stilled on his forehead and trembled. This was the moment she had feared. She loved him too much to walk away. She had given him too much of her heart to take back. She was his, and she was afraid.

Chapter 14

The pulsing rhythm of the band was well and truly under way. It was Mike's fortieth birthday and Leisa had hired a band and filled the courtyard of their home with white and crimson magnolia lights.

A blonde with a sultry voice belted out the latest pop hits. Amanda had taken over the cooking, sending Leisa out of the kitchen with a warning not to come back but to go and find her husband and make him happy. Bethany and her mother Estelle had come over early to help and now Estelle was sitting with Charlotte and baby Hayden in the huge courtyard between the house and the granny flat.

Scott was there with his latest ditzy blonde and had been snapped up by Amanda to help clear the tables for the dance. His shock at being given instructions was evident.

'Geez, mate, that Amanda is one bossy broad,' he said as he helped Mike place the chairs in a circle leaving the inner courtyard free for dancing. He looked appreciatively as the voluptuous Italian woman walked away, her hips swinging in time to the music.

'She's a gem. She has made our life easier,' said Mike.

Scott continued to stare after her, as she chatted with ease, her bejewelled hands moving expressively as she talked. Her hair was jet black and she wore a figure hugging red dress. Next to her his blonde companion paled.

'Too rich for your blood, Scott,' warned Jack as he gathered Chelsea into his arms for a spin around the dance floor. 'Apparently she left her husband when she discovered he was using their restaurant to launder money. She has changed her name and started a new life. Not your type mate.'

This only appeared to increase Scott's interest.

'I didn't think she looked like an 'Amanda',' he said, wandering over to ask for a dance. Leisa requested a slow number and melted into Mike's arms with a blissful smile.

Jack pulled Chelsea close and played with her neck. She had her hair up and she was wearing a black mini dress of de-lustred satin that moved with her. It was strapless and moulded to her curves alluringly. Jack looked into her emerald eyes and was so proud of her. She had noticed his tense mood of late and tonight he would talk to her. He would explain.

He loved her vibrant spirit, her courage. He knew she was wary and he still was afraid of frightening her away and he couldn't bear that. He wanted her close. Over the past months he had come to realise that his past relationships didn't go the distance because they lacked the fire and warmth that he shared with Chelsea. He had never felt the need to change his life. Suddenly his careful life seemed safe and empty.

Chelsea had been playful, light-hearted, warm and compassionate but had given nothing away of her feelings for him. Tonight he would ask some of the questions he longed to know.

Chelsea nestled into Jack's shoulder as he held her close. The red wine had relaxed her. She heard her name and looked up to Jack in a daze. But it wasn't Jack calling her name it was Mike and he held the portable phone towards her from the kitchen door. His face was full of concern. She followed Mike into the kitchen.

She heard the anguish and panic in her brother Terry's voice. The room became a blur and her legs shook. Mitch had been involved in a car accident and was in Tamworth Base Hospital fighting for his life. He had just been taken to surgery. Terry's voice broke and Chelsea went cold with fear.

There should be a law against enforced movie watching on coaches, Chelsea thought, as she held her pounding head. She closed her eyes but even then the searing soundtrack for the thriller movie hurt her head. She was weary and afraid for her brother.

Taking a coach to Tamworth had been the quickest solution to getting to her Mitch's side. How she wished that she could wave a magic wand and be with her brothers instantly but if there had been any magic in the world her sweet caring brother wouldn't be lying in an operating theatre right now. Her whole heart strained to be there.

The movie ended and the coach lights were dimmed. Even though she unable to relax Chelsea was glad of the silence until the woman in the seat behind her decided to strike up a lively conversation with her neighbour. The conversation intruded on her thoughts until she thought she would go mad.

It was after midnight and she desperately needed to compose herself. She would need to be strong for her brothers. She was the eldest and even though they had suffered the usual sibling hassles the boys had looked to her for leadership. They needed her and she would be there for them. She wiped her eyes as her own pain threatened to overwhelm her.

She could see Mitch with his wide smile when he and Terry had restored their first set of wheels—an old black sedan. She remembered him taking her to her Year 10 Formal when she had been stood up by Richard Stockdale only to find out when she got there that Richard had a bad case of chicken pox and sent his brother to partner her. Mitch had stayed and danced with her and had only gone home when he had interrogated Richard's brother and satisfied himself that Chelsea would come to no harm. She had been so amused when she got home to find both her brothers waiting up for her.

Bandages covered half of Mitch's dear familiar face. He was still unconscious and in the High Dependency Unit. He was only allowed one visitor at a time and Terry and his girlfriend Laura had been taking turns by his side. He had only been back from the theatre for two hours and was heavily sedated when Chelsea was shown into his room.

She felt so shocked and alone at his bedside. The cardiac monitor beeped regularly and every few minutes she heard the hiss of the blood pressure cuff filling to monitor his BP. Mitch was grey and still. He had been riding his motorcycle and his left leg had been amputated below the knee. He had also suffered a minor head trauma and internal injuries. He had received three units of blood and now had a transfusion of packed cells.

'He is lucky he was wearing a helmet,' said the sister who entered to check on him. 'The visor has cut his face and he has thirteen stitches.'

'Will he be alright?' said Chelsea her voice trembling.

'We don't know. He is stable for now. He has suffered fairly severe internal injuries. His spleen was damaged and they removed that in surgery. He has lost a lot of blood.'

The sister proceeded to write up the observations, reading them from the monitor.

'Are his observations okay, I mean, is he responding?'

The sister's look was gentle. His pulse if a bit rapid and blood pressure is down but it has improved in the last half hour. The next couple of days are crucial.' She paused. 'You know, the best thing you can do for him is to go home and rest. We will phone you but he will need his family to be rested when he wakes up.'

Sitting around the old kitchen table had been surreal. The sun came up and Laura pulled the kitchen curtains across as the early morning rays streamed into the room.

'No more coffee for you,' said Laura as Terry headed for his third cup. 'You need rest and that won't help.'

She firmly pushed him towards the bedroom and picked up Chelsea's suitcase.

'I can see why Terry is in love with you,' said Chelsea, smiling a weak smile.

'Has anyone notified Mum in the nursing home? Not that she will understand,' said Chelsea.

'Not formally, but you know how things are, word gets around. Some of the nurses work in both places. Many of them have two jobs.' said Laura.

'I will go and see her before anyone can talk to her.'

'But not now,' insisted Laura, 'you need rest. I will phone and warn the staff about upsetting her in case someone says the wrong thing and you will have to rest. You haven't had any sleep and I had a few hours last night.'

Chelsea was sure she wouldn't be able to sleep so she was surprised when she awoke three hours later. She was still suffering from shock and the feeling that this was a nightmare that she would wake from soon. She couldn't put off the visit to her mother any longer but she was unsure how much her mother would take in. She sent a text message to Jack as he would be at work now.

Her mother was sitting in a recliner looking out of the window when Chelsea arrived. Her mauve tinted hair was decorously arranged and she sat meekly with her hands folded in her lap.

'Hello Mum,' Chelsea said, 'It's me, Chelsea.'

'Hello dear, do I know you?' her mother said politely. This wasn't going to be easy. Chelsea went to sit in the chair opposite and Iris instantly jumped.

'Don't sit on Edward dear,' she said and Chelsea turned to find a small teddy bear on the seat. The tears began to flow as Chelsea realised her mother was in another world and any chance of connecting with her today was small. Saddened that she couldn't face this with her own mother she felt a sense of how bizarre the situation was.

'Don't cry dear, have you lost your friends, do you want me to call the nurse?' Iris was becoming a little agitated. Chelsea had always found visits with her mother to be difficult but today was so much worse because of Mitch's accident. She composed herself.

'How are you today Iris,' she asked. Her mother settled back into the chair and became calmer.

'I am quite good today dear, and you?'

'Could be better,' said Chelsea honestly. 'What are you going to do today?' Maybe if her mother was comfortable she might have a period of lucidity and be able to recognise Chelsea. It didn't seem likely but Chelsea remembered that if she reminisced it might trigger something.

'I am going to help mum bottle tomatoes. My sister Anna has run off as usual leaving me all the work,' said Iris with a sigh.

'Have you done much bottling this spring?'

'We have just finished the peaches and mum wants to get onto the apples next because dad is so fond of his apple pies.'

'That's good mum...Iris,' Chelsea said with a tearful sigh.

A young nurse with thick auburn hair piled on her head came into the room.

'Iris, are you going down to Bingo this morning?' she asked.

Chelsea walked her mother down to the therapy room where walking frames were lined up in the hall outside. An assortment of older residents sat inside at tables waiting on an enthusiastic woman with short permed hair to set up Bingo. Several of the ladies beckoned Iris and she went and sat with them giving Chelsea a confused wave.

The auburn haired nurse greeted Chelsea and that gave Chelsea the opportunity to ask how her mother was faring.

'She is having a good day today. Some days she is very anxious and agitated. Sometimes she wanders at night but she hasn't for a while. You're the daughter from Sydney? The preschool teacher?' she asked.

'Yes, I came up last night because my brother Mitch had a motorcycle accident and he is critical. I had hoped to connect with mum and explain but she doesn't know me.'

'Just give her a few days and she might remember. She sometimes knows the boys. I am so sorry to hear about your brother, he's one of twins isn't he.'

'Yes, we are very upset, he is in the Base Hospital and we won't know how he will do for days. He had his leg amputated and he suffered internal injuries.'

'He will get good care there and there is a rehabilitation centre that operates out of Johnson House next to the hospital so he will be well cared for. Don't feel bad about your mother; she couldn't help the situation even if she does remember for a short time. It is hard when you have to be the parent to your own mother.'

'We just hope Mitch makes it at this stage.'

The nurse put a reassuring arm around Chelsea's shoulder.

'Just take care of yourself and look after your brothers. We will take care of your mother. I hope everything goes well. When things get a bit better you might be able to connect with your mum. But don't worry if you can't. We have a lot of patients like her and it is hard for the families. You have to remember that your mother hasn't rejected you by forgetting, her mind has deteriorated.'

Chelsea was warmed by the sympathy of the nurse and her common sense approach. She went back to the car that Terry had given her for the duration of her stay. Alicia would arrive that evening from Indonesia. They would be all together in the family home again. Except for Mitch.

She sat in the car and searched in her bag for her mobile phone. She was missing Jack so much it was a physical pain. He had offered to drive her last night but she had worried that he had been ill in Hong Kong and had piles of work to catch up on in the office because of his ten days overseas.

She checked her messages. There was a text message, 'take care, talk tonight, Jack xx'. She looked at her watch, it was 1 pm. If she was lucky she might catch Jack at lunch. The company secretary Alison told her that he was in a meeting and wouldn't be available for the rest of the day. She went back to the hospital and her vigil by Mitch's bedside. She and Terry took turns to sit beside him when they were allowed between his nursing cares.

Alicia arrived at six o'clock in the evening and Chelsea and Terry welcomed her with open arms. In typical Alicia style she wanted to bluster into the middle of everything but one look at Mitch had her sitting in the High Dependency waiting room subdued and shocked.

'He looks so strange, not like our brother at all,' she said wiping her hand across her forehead. Her black hair was short and spiked and she was immaculately made up.

Chelsea reached out and held her hand, stroking it gently. 'I know sis.'

'He is the best of us you know, the sweetest nature even given,' said Alicia. 'It's so unfair.'

'Yes, it is,' responded Chelsea. The two women sat and talked, then took turns by his side until at eight o'clock they were politely told that they could come back in the morning as early as they liked. Alicia had requested to stay by his side all night but the nurse kindly told her that that was not allowed and explained that if everyone did that they would not be able to do their jobs.

They both turned on their mobile phones in the car park and Chelsea drove the battered Corolla back to the house.

'Being back here without Mitch and mum is so unreal,' said Alicia later. Laura was taking care of them all, refusing them coffee and making creamy hot chocolates so they would sleep well. She had her own flat in town and had to work early in the morning so she soon left the three siblings.

Chelsea went and sat on the porch swing and Jack phoned at nine. He asked after Mitch and said that he wished he could be there with her. She told him of Mitch's condition and said that there would be more news in a few days.

'Alicia arrived a couple of hours ago,' Chelsea said.

'And how is Mother Superior, lording it over you all?' he questioned using their nickname for Alicia.

Chelsea let out a tinkling laugh. 'What a good memory you have Stretch. She isn't yet but I'm sure she will get into stride sometime soon.' Chelsea talked about the shock of seeing Mitch and then asked about Leisa and Mike.

'They send their love and Leisa said that if you need to talk to ring her anytime, but you know that already,' he said. I want your love, thought Chelsea.

'We are seeing the neurologist in the morning for a progress report, so I will ring her then. We saw the surgeon today and he said that the bleeding has resolved and the surgery went well so we just have to wait to see how his body responds. They have him heavily sedated. There was some brain swelling and they put medication to deal with that in his IV. Tomorrow's news will be key.'

'I hope you get good news,' he said. 'I put your car in for a service by the way, might as well get it done while you are away.'

'Thank you,' she said, deeply appreciating the gesture.

'Well you know us males, we feel helpless without a physical problem to solve.'

'I am feeling very helpless myself, just looking at Mitch lying there.' Tell me you love me, she thought willing him to say the words.

'Well, sweet Scheherazade, I will let you out of your storytelling contract for tonight and wish you sweet dreams; of me,. Jack said his heart bursting with love for his brave Scheherazade. I won't tell you of my love now, you won't trust the words.

When she woke in the morning Alicia had gone to see their mother in the nursing home. Chelsea moaned inwardly. Terry told her over breakfast that Alicia had taken the car earlier. Chelsea worried that Alicia would confront Iris and make things worse with her attitude of making everyone 'face reality'.

Alicia was quiet and tense when she returned and merely said that the aged care hostel supervisor wanted to have a case conference while they were available. Chelsea left the subject alone and they went to the hospital and spent the day much as they had the one before and this became the pattern for the week.

One thing the two sisters shared in common was that neither of them wanted to eat. Only Laura's care and bossiness had them sitting down for meals at all. The other thing they shared was their dark anxiety for their brother that hung over them like a pall. At the end of the fourth day they received the wonderful news that Mitch was conscious and even though he was still having strong pain relief he was alert enough to talk to them.

When they arrived at the High Dependency Unit the sister allowed all three siblings in for a brief time.

'Good grief girls, you look worse than me,' were Mitch's first croaky words. He was rewarded with three wide matching smiles. Then they all talked at once and Mitch rolled his eyes theatrically.

'That's more like it,' he murmured. 'Now I know I have the right family.'

Mitch's recovery went ahead in leaps and bounds from then on. The surgical team told the family of the long months of physiotherapy that Mitch would need and three days later he was transferred to the Rehab Ward and fitted with a prosthetic foot.

'Mitch is going to need a manual car,' said Terry as they ate a traditional roast dinner on the Sunday after Mitch was admitted to the Rehab Ward. 'That means the sports car will have to go.'

'He will hate that, he loves that car,' said Alicia. 'I remember how long it took him to do it up.'

'Well, he has told me to get rid of it. He is being realistic, so unlike him,' said Terry.

'Yes,' said Alicia, 'The drama queen in him has been noticeably absent.'

The phone rang shrilly and Alicia answered it. It was Jack.

Chelsea stood looking out of the familiar kitchen window and heard the words she had heard so many times before in her childhood.

'I have resigned from my position.' Jack's words flew around her head and the rest of the conversation was blurring as she tried to come to terms with this upheaval.

'What will you do?' she asked suddenly afraid. This couldn't be happening, not stable calm Jack. How could she have missed this? A strong sense of déjà vu overcame her. She had been in this very kitchen when her father had come home and told the family that he was leaving everything familiar and safe and taking them with him. She watched the lace curtains flutter in the breeze. She looked out onto the small orchard. She had stood here before and heard these same words.

'I don't know yet. I am looking at some options. I am going to visit my father in the country. I have been thinking about slowing down,' Jack continued, unaware of the panic he was causing at the other end of the phone.

'I can't do this Jack. I have been there before. I can't live a life of insecurity.'

'But Scheherazade, you haven't let me explain.'

'I'm sorry Jack, I know how this goes. I can't do this.'

All the misery of the past week that had been bottled up inside her came flowing out as she ran into her room. The grief and worry that she had suppressed for her brother joined the crushing disappointment of facing the meaning of Jack's words. She was heartbroken.

Chapter 15

'Just how is it possible to fall asleep on a motorcycle?' Alicia asked Mitch on his first evening home after his discharge from hospital.

'I wouldn't expect you to understand, Miss Princess and the Pea,' said Mitch referring to the nick name they had given Alicia due to her constant moaning and inability to sleep unless she was lying down. He bit into the almond chocolate biscuits that Chelsea had made. 'These are great Sis, it's good to be home again.'

'No, seriously Mitchell Prentiss. I want an answer,' demanded Alicia.

'Ooh I'm in trouble. The Princess is calling me my full name,' muttered Mitch around the mouthful of biscuit. 'I may have to eat all of these. Hospital food is shocking.'

'Help yourself darling,' said Chelsea handing him the baking tray.

'Don't give him the whole tray Chels,' protested Terry, 'he'll only make a pig of himself.'

'No one is listening to me,' shrieked Alicia.

'I can't believe after a decade of being grownups we are right back to the same conversations,' said Chelsea.

'Will somebody please tell me how anybody could fall asleep on a motorcycle!' barked Alicia. They all burst out laughing. It was such a relief to have Mitch home. Alicia was flying back to Singapore the following day.

'I don't remember calling Alicia the Princess and the Pea but I remember we called Chelsea 'Sleeping Beauty', because she could fall asleep anywhere.'

'Well she isn't 'Sleeping Beauty' at the moment!' muttered Alicia. 'She is more 'Cry Me a River'.'

'What is she talking about Chels? What have I missed out on?' asked Mitch.

'Prince Charming is lost and hasn't hacked his way through the vines around the castle and so 'Sleeping Beauty' is inconsolable,' said Alicia.

'Is nothing sacred in this family?' groaned Chelsea.

'No!' shouted all three at once.

It was true. Chelsea had missed Jack more than she could say and she had tried to hide her pain but Alicia and Terry had known and asked her about it. She had refused to talk about it and had spent her time scrubbing the house and cooking for the boys. She had been unable to enjoy her food very much as her appetite had disappeared and she had lost a little weight.

'I want to hear all about this 'Prince Charming' Chels, but first I will tell all,' Mitch said.

'The drama queen is back,' said Alicia.

'I was on my way to a funeral,' he began. All three began to talk at once and he put up his hand theatrically and waited for silence.

'As I said; I was on my way to a funeral, thankfully not my own funeral, ha ha. I was going to Aunt Dulcie's funeral, you know, dad's only sister. I have visited her regularly for years—ever since we went overseas together about seven years ago, you remember? She is an old dear; I should say *was*. I had worked all night on old man Carson's tractor and had only had two hours sleep. Anyway, I managed to fall asleep on the bike. At least that is the best I can work out because no other vehicles were involved.'

They were all silent now. The wrecked motorcycle was in the twins' workshop and they had all been shocked to see it.

'I had a visitor in hospital, Mr Cradden, Aunt Dulcie's solicitor.'

None of them were surprised at this as they had expected Mitch to inherit something from their aunt. 'Well the upshot of that visit was that Aunt Dulcie left Granddad's property to be shared between the four of us.'

This was a shock to both the girls. Apparently Mitch had already told Terry but had waited until now to tell the girls.

'Terry and I would like to buy out your share of this house,' Mitch said to Alicia and Chelsea. We are very grateful that you have allowed us to live here as the youngest and weakest.' A cheeky grin was plastered over his face. 'There will be enough left over to pay out the mortgage on your flat Chelsea and enough for you and Lance to put down on a house, Alicia. Terry and I will be able to build a bigger workshop and set up business here.'

This was good news for them all but Chelsea couldn't shift the feeling of loss over Jack. She felt so connected to him. But it was better to end now rather than years down the track when he decided that he wanted something else or someone else. If only he had told her that he loved her. She would have had a reference point for understanding; or a reason to hope.

At least now she would have the security she craved by completely owning her flat. She thought of her brothers and Alicia and was grateful for family. The amount that Mitch had said they would receive was far greater than her remaining mortgage. She should take a holiday and get away for a while. She was returning to Sydney in a few days. She had requested a month of compassionate leave and she had ten days left. Jack had sent text messages and left phone messages with Alicia but Chelsea had not responded to them. The sense of aching loss gnawed at her stomach.

'I'll buy your car Mitch,' she said, in a moment of clarity. She would sell the little two door hatch when she got back to Sydney. She thought about the feeling of freedom she would have when she drove back to Sydney with the top of the sports car down and the wind in her hair.

'You sure Chels?' asked Mitch.

'I'm sure,' she said with conviction.

'Done,' said Mitch, 'and now you must tell us about Prince Charming. Don't hold it all in, darling. That's what you always do.' He sounded like their mother.

'I think 'Prince Charming' hacked his way through the vines but she threw him out because the wicked witch put a spell on her,' said Terry. He had taken several calls from Jack and wondered what was going on.

'Oh Terry, remind me to never let you tell my future children bedtime stories. Really,' said Alicia.

So Chelsea told them about winning the prize and her first impressions of Jack. She told them about her wonderful week in Surfer's Paradise and their days with Jemima and the soap opera cast. She told how he had sorted her contract. She told them about his Jack Sparrow act.

'This guy sounds like a peach,' said Mitch, frowning in confusion.

She told them that he had taught her to swim and that he had let her think he was employed by the television station so that he could see more of her.

'So this Jack changed his schedule so that he could go on holiday with you and get to know you?' questioned Mitch. 'What sort of a beast does *that?*' he said in mock horror and then mouthed at the others—'is she for real.'

'So what on earth is wrong with the man then Chels?' Alicia was amazed. 'This man sounds like a prince.'

'He started saying all the same things dad did, I won't ever live like that again,' muttered Chelsea. 'I can't believe that I was here standing in the same place listening to the same words. I never want to feel that way again.'

'What the hell did he say Chels?' asked Mitch. 'Has he got another woman?'

'No, it wasn't that, he has left his job, he's unsure about his future and that, along with the fact that he has never told me that he loved me, has left me feeling insecure.'

'People change their jobs all the time Chels,' said Alicia, gently touching Chelsea's arm. 'Are you sure you're not making a mountain out of a mole hill.'

'You're not just running away are you Chels?' said Terry.

'You didn't give the man a fair hearing if you ask me darling,' said Mitch.

'Whose side are you on?' Chelsea grumbled, unwilling to concede.

'Yours,' all three shouted.

'But give the man a hearing,' said Mitch, 'after all, he may be on your side too.'

Jack would never in his wildest dreams have imagined seeing his father in gum boots and moleskins wandering around an orchard. He was wearing an Akubra hat and looked so thoroughly at home as he showed Jack his apple trees. Jack had been in Stanthorpe with his father, James and his wife Elise for the past week.

The cool mountain air ruffled his hair as it curled over his collar. It felt good to be without a suit and tie. But better still he was glad of this time with his father. Chelsea had been right about him needing to make an effort to reconnect.

For the past few days he had just slept and ate. The virus he had contracted overseas had affected him more than he thought. But the ache he had for Chelsea had outlasted the virus and would certainly plague him for the rest of his life, he thought with a wry smile. She was unique; a breath of fresh air in his convenient life.

He finally broached the subject of his sadness and was surprised at his father's wisdom when he confided his love for Chelsea and her response to his news about resigning.

'Give her time, son, she sounds like the real thing. When she has time to think she'll come around. Let her know that you have both your feet on the ground and that she can trust you.'

'But she won't even listen to me or return my calls.'

'You're a lawyer, you'll think of something,' his father had said with a knowing smile.

'When did you get to be so all-wise?' mumbled Jack.

'The minute you stopped knowing everything,' said James, 'and not before time I might add. It was probably only yesterday.' He threw his head back and roared with laughter. 'Every father waits for the day. You will wait for it too with your own son.'

My son. Jack liked the thought of that more than he would admit. He imagined a cheeky boy with caramel curls and a daughter with straight hair and a serious thoughtful face. Talking with his father had given him hope.

'I hope that my marriage break up hasn't soured you, son. I would hate to think that. I have waited to let you come to me when you were ready but I was wrong to do that. I should have sat down with you and helped you through it. I let guilt stand in my way. I hope you can forgive me.' James blue searching eyes asked for a new beginning with his son.

'I should have come sooner, I let pride get in my way,' said Jack.

'It's usually a mistake to leave things unsaid with loved ones. Your mother and I made that mistake. I hope our children learn from our mistakes.'

'Elise is a lovely woman. I am glad you are happy. I want that for myself.'

'Then you will have to take a risk. Put your thoughts into words. Don't let misunderstanding keep you apart. Life's too short.'

'It is easier to write a contract or a deposition than to tell a woman you love her,' murmured Jack.

'Then do that,' said James.

'What?'

'Write a deposition,' said James, 'a deposition of love.'

'I am so in love with this rocking chair,' said Chelsea as she cradled her tiny godson in her lap. She was sitting with Leisa in the courtyard. Leisa was kneading dough for pizza bases on the outdoor table.

'I can't believe you dumped Jack because he sounded like your father,' said Leisa.

'I thought motherhood might have mellowed you but you still know how to aim for the jugular don't you?' sputtered Chelsea.

'It is my duty as best friend,' said Leisa, continuing to pummel the dough. 'It is what I signed on for when we were three and I take my kindred spirit responsibilities very seriously. You're crazy.'

'He could have said he loved me,' said Chelsea defending herself mutinously.

'If he had told you right when your brother had been in an accident you wouldn't have believed him. He's not stupid. He knows you have trust issues.'

'He sounded just like dad.'

'Tell me again, just so I have it straight. Just which words sounded like your father?'

'Let me see—'resigned', 'pursuing options', 'don't know', 'country life'—those words.'

'And you condemn him on that! You could have heard him out.'

'I was afraid. I was afraid to hear more.'

'So you imagined the rest, well, congratulations your credentials as an author of fiction are confirmed.'

'That's harsh.'

'I love you; I'm your best friend. Remember when you talked to me about giving Mike a chance. This is the watershed moment.'

'What do you mean, the watershed moment?' Chelsea was confused. Really it was hard to keep up with the twists and turns of Leisa's mind when she got started.

'Do you remember early in the pregnancy with Hayden that I panicked? I had so many miscarriages that I was sure I was in trouble again.'

'How could I forget, you had lost four babies at 12 weeks and every time you got that far you were terrified.'

'Yes, and you told me that I couldn't let my past experiences keep me from the dream of having my own child come true. You helped me through that time and now look at you holding the beautiful outcome.'

Tears pricked Chelsea's eyes.

'You know I'm right. Give him a chance. Did you know he has still been going to the preschool on Tuesdays to see Duncan?' Jack had begun coming to the preschool every Tuesday to pick Chelsea up from work and take her to the Italian pizzeria on Lane Cove River.

'Really?'

'*Really!*' said Leisa. 'That doesn't sound like a man who is untrustworthy. And take care with my son. If you keep up that energetic rocking you will wear his lunch.' Chelsea slowed the rocking motion. Oh dear, I *am* agitated, she thought.

Chelsea was a nervous as a gazelle with a lion nearby. She sat taking deep breaths outside of Jack's apartment building toying with the key to his townhouse. It was early on a Sunday morning. She hadn't slept. She had written notes and rehearsed what she would say knowing that if she didn't prepare what she wanted to say she might just throw herself into Jack's arms and howl like a baby.

She had dressed to impress with a red dress that Alicia had told her would be a crime to leave behind when the two sisters had gone shopping together. She looked at her notes. She had to get this right, she had avoided risk too much of her life. She didn't want to be like her mother, always letting things go and never asking for what she wanted in life.

She had been stunned during the case conference about her mother to find out that her mother had suffered a 'nervous breakdown' in her twenties before she had met their father. The information had come out when the aged care supervisor had discussed her medical history. She and Alicia had been shocked. Apparently Iris had been hospitalised for several weeks at the time. When the young supervisor described the conditions of the wards back then they had been deeply affected by the ordeal their mother had endured. Perhaps this explained why their mother was so desperate to keep the status quo, to avoid rocking the boat of their family life. Maybe this is what drove her to follow their father without question or complaint.

Resolutely grabbing her purse and the key Chelsea swung out of the car and went into the building. She said hello to Annalisa the apartment manager who was in her office and took the lift to the third floor. She thought Annalisa looked surprised to see her but brushed that aside.

She swung the door open and was stunned to find that the apartment was eerily bare. There was no sign of anything apart from the chrome and glass furniture that she detested. She held the door jamb for support.

'Chelsea, I tried to catch you. Jack moved out last week.' It was Annalisa.

'But the furniture is still here,' said Chelsea perplexed. 'Where did he go?'

'The furniture belongs with the apartment,' said Annalisa, 'and you know I couldn't divulge his new address even if I knew it, which I don't. Sorry Chelsea. I will need the key from you though.'

'Did he say anything?' Chelsea felt lost.

'No, he just left a huge bouquet for the staff, sorry.'

Burning with embarrassment Chelsea handed over the key and left the building. She drove with the top down trying desperately to fight the inevitable tears. She was chilled and shivering when she arrived on Geraldine's doorstep.

'Come in pet, you're freezing,' said Geraldine, throwing the door wide and enveloping Chelsea in a warm embrace.

'Geraldine, what have you done?' Chelsea saw the cast on her leg and the walking frame that Geraldine had discarded by the door.

'I broke my damn ankle chasing next door's dog away from my orchids in the greenhouse. My Bert grew those and I love them.' Geraldine looked pale and tired.

'Let me make you a cup of tea,' volunteered Chelsea as she headed towards the kitchen. She made the tea in the pot with Geraldine's instructions. She loved the English tea making traditions.

'Thank goodness for a proper cup of tea, those boys give me those awful teabags. I can't abide them!' complained Geraldine. Chelsea looked up at the mention of the 'boys'. 'And don't go thinking that I will tell you anything about Jack when you don't have the courage to talk to him yourself,' she chastised.

'I have been trying to find him to talk to him. I should have given him the chance. I know that now. I'm so afraid, Geraldine.'

'You don't seem afraid of anything Chelsea Prentiss. I have high hopes for you,' said Geraldine. 'Can you light the fire for me pet? It's freezing in here. I feel so useless with this damn leg.'

While Chelsea set about preparing the kindling and lighting the open fire in the dining room that adjoined the kitchen Geraldine plotted. She relaxed back in the rocker recliner, a subtle smile playing on her lips. Honestly young people these days. She would just have to give a helping hand. If it hadn't been for her old nanny Betty, back in England arranging for Bert to be in the park after she had tearfully told him she couldn't see him again they would never have ended up together. She would have missed out on the love of her life. She gripped the arm of the chair fiercely. These two people deserved to be happy.

'Who is looking after you Geraldine? Did the hospital organise a community nurse?'

Geraldine put on her most helpless expression. God forgive her for her deception.

'They did pet,' she said with her wide eyes innocent, 'but the poor girl's mother died. Not that there is much to do really, I'll be alright.' She threw her hands out in a gesture of resignation.

'Well, I can come and stay with you; I have another week of compassionate leave. Mitch recovered so well and was chafing at all of us 'meddling'.'

'Are you sure, dear?' said Geraldine with a satisfied smile. 'That will put my mind at ease.' Geraldine made a mental note to phone the community health service and cancel the nurse.

Several days later Geraldine and Chelsea had their heads together at the kitchen table sorting through photographs for

Geraldine's memoirs when there was a knock at the door. Chelsea was on her feet instantly. She was used to running around to answer the phone and the door for Geraldine. She had bought Geraldine a portable phone on one of her shopping expeditions so Geraldine could chatter with her many friends.

There was a man in some sort of uniform at the door with a parcel. Chelsea signed for it and wandered back to the sitting room.

'It's a delivery. Were you expecting anything?' she said handing it to Geraldine. Geraldine frowned. Really, what was wrong with Jack, she had told him three days ago that Chelsea was here and was pining for him. Male pride, she thought as she looked at the parcel. 'It's for you dear,' she said to Chelsea. What was that boy up to?

Chelsea looked confused. She opened the parcel and there was a large brown envelope that had her name on it and another parcel wrapped in brown paper.

'Curiouser and curiouser,' she mumbled, opening the envelope.

Inside there was a typewritten sheet of paper with an official letterhead and the words Deposition for Chelsea Prentiss at the top. She read on,

Renshaw & Devon
Solicitors & Attorneys
Suite 3, Macquarie House
Settlement Road
CASTLE HILL NSW

I, Jack Sparrow, Captain and Pirate of the High Seas and many bold adventures, wish to throw myself at the mercy of the court and plead, not for my freedom, but for my imprisonment. Imprison me in your arms. Sentence me to life; life with you. You are the judge of my heart. You are the jury that decides my future. I love you.

I have been misjudged by this court. I left my ship, not to roam and be free, but to settle on dry land, to find a place away from the plundering and 'convenience' of my former life. I have not left my calling; I have found it.

It was signed and dated.

'Oh my goodness,' she said as she hastily tore the wrapping to find an adorable giraffe with a bandage over one ear. Pinned to the giraffe was a handwritten message. Chelsea fondled the giraffe's carefully bandaged ear and the bandage fell off to reveal a beautiful diamond solitaire ring attached to the ear.

> ps. Please accept Gerald the Giraffe. I know the giraffe you loved when you were a child had a missing ear but I couldn't bear to cut the ear off so I just bandaged it.
>
> Receipt of said Giraffe will hold the receiver liable for the life of said giraffe and the sender and will be considered a legally binding contract with the sender for the rest of our lives.
>
> Marry me, Chelsea.
>
> pps. I will be waiting in the greenhouse.

Joyfully Chelsea ran outside to find Jack leaning on the doorway to the greenhouse with his hands in his jean pockets. He wore the lazy smile she had come to love. She was suddenly shy. The 'deposition' had answered all her doubts. She had noticed the letterhead, 'Renshaw and Devon' and realised that he had set up a law practice nearby in Castle Hill.

'Hey Stretch,' she murmured, waving the deposition at him. 'You think this gets you out of trouble?'

'Yep.'

'Says everything you want to say, does it?'

'Yep.'

'Man of few words today, aren't we?'

'Yep.'

'So who is this from? You or Jack Sparrow?' she questioned saucily.

'Come here and kiss me, my sweet Scheherazade. Stop with the questions and give me an answer.'

She gave him a lingering kiss. His arms encircled her, drawing her to him. 'Do you want that in writing, Stretch?'

'Maybe I better, in case you run scared again.'

She handed him the scrunched note that she had carried for weeks with what she wanted to say written on it. Jack looked at the note perplexed and then let out a roar of a laugh. Chelsea had written a page of indecipherable words and had crossed them all out except the words 'I love you Jack.'

'Now that's my kind of answer,' he said; his laughter rumbled through her body as he held her close.

'So does that mean you will become Mrs Jack Devon?' he asked when his kisses had turned her to jelly. She clung to him for support.

'Yep.'

'Good answer, you're learning.'

'I do love you Jack,' she whispered into his shoulder.

'I have loved you from the minute I saw your funny routine in the Arabian Nights tent. You have captured my heart. I was afraid I had lost you.'

'I thought you were getting restless like my father—always seeking greener pastures.'

'I just want to choose the kind of law practice that I do. I met up with my old university lecturer and he was looking for a junior partner. It was so good to feel excited about work again. I had lost that. And I fell in love with you. You challenged my thinking. I wanted more. I wanted you. My constant travel would be hard on a family; our family.'

'Oh, I have been thick haven't I? Assuming that you wanted to travel more, when you actually wanted to travel less. I was so upset about Mitch and I needed to hear that you loved me.'

'I didn't want to tell you over the phone when you were in the middle of a family crisis. I didn't think you would believe me and I didn't want to mess it up.' He drew her closer to him and kissed her face. 'But I intend to tell you for the rest of my life. I love you.'

'I just heard the word 'leaving' and I panicked. I didn't want to give you the chance to hurt me like my father had. Why did you leave your apartment?'

'I was so tired of living in a high rise in the city with no warmth and sense of home. I found that with you and I want to marry you and raise a family in a real home where the kids have room to grow and run.'

'Where are you staying now?'

'Scott has a six month overseas contract and asked me to look after his house on the beach. When he comes back I hope to have a contract of a different kind with you, my sweet Scheherazade.' His lingering hungry kisses drove all thought of conversation away.

'We had better go and tell Geraldine,' she said when they reluctantly drew apart.

'I think she will already know. After all it was she who told me where to find you.'

'Scheming old woman,' muttered Chelsea, loving Geraldine for her intervention.

'Let's go and tell her that she has new outfit to buy for our wedding,' said Jack putting his arm firmly around Chelsea and taking her inside to an expectant Geraldine who was sitting by the warmth of the fire.

Their beaming smiles told her everything she needed to know

and she gave them an answering smile, rising to hug them. When they gave her all their good news she congratulated them and said, 'I should think so.'

Chapter 16

Jack looked towards the back of the church. All eyes were scanning the arched doorway to the little sandstone chapel, waiting for the bride to appear. He adjusted his white bow tie for the hundredth time. The coal black tuxedo was snug fitting. The tails were a bit over the top but he didn't care.

The bridal march had begun and Scott was nervously fidgeting by his side. Jack gave him a reassuring smile. He knew how he felt. He caught Chelsea's eye as she stood beside Leisa and Mike, cradling her pregnant belly lovingly. His beautiful Scheherazade. They had come so far together.

He heard Scott suck in a breath as his bride Amanda stepped slowly towards him. She was wearing a slinky sheath dress that was made from Italian lace over lustrous satin and the V neck line was decorated with tiny seed pearls. She looked amazing with her shiny black hair waving down her back and her face lit up with a radiant smile.

In Jack's eyes she would never compare to Chelsea. He remembered his own wedding day over a year ago now when Chelsea had walked down the aisle with her twin brothers on either side of her. When asked 'Who gives this woman?' they had started the congregation laughing with their enthusiastic, 'We do!' Jack smiled at the memory.

He noticed Chelsea patting the knee rug around Geraldine as she sat in the wheelchair next to her. How he adored his caring wife. Geraldine chafed at her fussing and waved her away with an imperious hand. She was frailer now and was living in a nursing home near them. She had been like a mother to him when his own mother had died and he was pleased that she was part of their lives.

Geraldine had made the decision to move to the nursing home gracefully and had asked Jack and Chelsea if they would be interested in buying her home. They had been thrilled to grant her request.

He wouldn't tell her, but Chelsea had a paint smudge on her hand from repainting the guest room as a nursery. It reminded him of the time she had green gunk left on her face when he had rescued her from her pampering experience on the set of 'Daydream Island'. Now there was a permanent reminder of that time with both of them painted into the mural at Le Cirque.

The congregation was laughing as Scott reached out for Amanda before the celebrant had asked 'Who gives this woman?' Scott shrugged his shoulders and refused to release Amanda from his arm. He had fought long and hard for this woman. She hadn't made it easy. She hadn't falling into his arms like the legion of ditzy socialites before her. Jack remembered how hard it had been to impress Chelsea and how wonderful it had been when he had been sure of her love.

He felt blessed and grateful. He had been thrilled last week when Chelsea's novella 'Two Hearts, One Suitcase' based on Geraldine's love story had received a literary award. His own law practice with his tutor, John Renshaw from his Uni days, had flourished. Jack had no regrets about leaving corporate law to set up the practice with John. There were no more overseas trips and he relished the time with Chelsea especially as they waited for their daughter to arrive.

The sun shone fiercely through the Jacaranda trees outside the little stone chapel as the wedding party posed for their photos. Chelsea sat with Geraldine watching Mike try to shepherd Hayden's wayward steps as he ran gleefully away with his awkward toddler gait.

Jack caught her eye and smiled. He looked so handsome and self-assured in his dark suit. A rush of love for him overwhelmed her. She patted Geraldine's hand and thought about how her fears had nearly kept them apart.

She remembered his earnest eyes as he had sought to make her understand that his love for her could be trusted. She had met his father and his wife and found him to be a warm and funny man like his son. She thought of the time wasted between the two men and determined that she would never run away again but would find the courage to talk things out; to listen.

She thought of her first impressions of Jack and wondered how she could have ever thought of him as dull or spoiled. His playful smile and intelligent eyes still had the power to mesmerize her.

She felt a sharp pain. Not now baby, let me have this wedding. But another pain followed straight after. Jack saw her grab her stomach and was instantly at her side.

Chelsea looked down at the tiny perfect yawning face of their darling daughter. Jack stood puffed up with fatherly pride beside her. She had accepted the humorous jibes of the nurses who teased her when she hadn't wanted Jack to leave her side in the labour ward.

'She's like this all the time,' he had said as Chelsea clutched his white shirt sleeve as wave after wave of contraction seized her. 'Never lets me out of her sight. Ouch.'

The nurse took baby Sheri from Chelsea and placed her in her proud father's waiting arms.

'She looks like such a quiet little thing,' remarked the nurse.

Chelsea looked straight into Jack's clear laughing eyes.

'You know what they say about first impressions,' said Jack.

Beneath the Flame Tree

Kate Reid is alone in the world. She has forged a place for herself by running 'Belle Maison' a Bed & Breakfast in the home her father left her. When one of her guests, the secretive Eleanor Mansfield dies suddenly she finds a letter addressed to Michael Randall, and a photo of a young boy attached. Who is Michael Randall and how is he connected to the dead woman? How will she deliver this letter? And just who is the handsome guest who seems so determined to help her with the B & B?

~~~

An icy southerly wind seeped under the French doors into the small room and the blue of the sky was obscured by dark threatening clouds. The day had started poorly and showed no sign of improving.

At least the police had left, after taking copious notes; giving Leisa the all clear to tidy the room. Maybe things would get back to normal now. It wasn't every day a client died quietly on the floor at the *Belle Maison Bed & Breakfast*.

Eleanor Mansfield had left the world at that morning in the same way she had lived her latter days; without fuss or fanfare. The place had buzzed with activity; ambulance, police and the local doctor.

Then everyone had gone as quickly as they came, asking where the nearest take-away could be found. Except for Dr Grainger who was pleasantly ensconced at her kitchen table being waited on by two of her elderly clients, Sissy and Celia Fenn.

Leisa Reid wiped off the sweat that was streaming down her forehead with the back of a grimy hand. Her fine blonde hair was tied in a ponytail with a cleaning rag, making her look younger than her 27 years. Wisps of hair escaped, framing her dainty face. She knelt on the floor; scrubbing the timber boards distractedly.

The silence of the morning was broken by the rhythmic sounds of the scrubbing brush on timber and the gentle scraping of the flame tree branches on the bay window.

On the love seat under the windows, Banjo the kitten, was stealthily eyeing his errant tail as it flicked across his line of vision with the intensity of a lion cub stalking its prey. Leisa sighed, at least the blasted cat had stopped tipping the rubbish bin over and chasing the papers around like a frantic one-man hockey team.

At times like these she wondered what had possessed her to turn her spacious home into a B & B. Three policemen, two ambulance men, a doctor and a body bag were too much for anyone before 8 am.

Leisa sighed, it was three hours since the police had left and she still had to pack Eleanor's clothes and the rest of her belongings. Looking at her watch she realised it was nearly time to prepare lunch for her guests.

Leisa groaned as she struggled to her feet and rubbed her lower back, but she only had to clean out the bedside table and the room would be finished. Then she could try to figure out what to do with Eleanor Mansfield's meagre possessions.

She opened the top drawer. There was a small old fashioned biscuit tin with the lid beside it as if Eleanor had been looking at it just moments ago.

Leisa shivered. The room was cold. She would be glad to be rid of the sad pall this woman had worn like a shroud.

Feeling like an intruder she removed the tin. Inside was a small key. There was also an envelope that had a photograph attached with an old metal paperclip. The photo was of a boy who looked no more than ten.

The envelope was sealed and there was a name 'Michael Randall' written in thick manly scrawl. The writing was unlike Eleanor's feathery script.

Who was Michael Randall? What on earth did that envelope contain, she wondered? And what was Leisa supposed to do about it? She sunk to the floor with an exhausted sigh.

Only six months before Eleanor Mansfield, Leisa's youngest resident, had arrived at 'Belle Maison' with secrets; and she'd died taking them with her.

Leisa was just cleaning up after the evening meal when she heard the sound of flying gravel. Only her best friend, Chelsea, drove like that. She welcomed the distraction of Chelsea's visit.

'Ooh, I love a good mystery,' chirped Chelsea when Leisa finished her tale.

Leisa sighed. She wished she had Chelsea's spirit of adventure, so far this 'mystery' had only caused her grief.

'I wish I knew what to do about this letter,' said Leisa, a little more vehemently than she intended. She pointed at the letter as if it were poison.

'It's only a letter Leisa, really! I am supposed to be the drama queen. It won't bite.'

Leisa felt a pang for the boy in the picture, whoever he was. This whole episode was bringing back the sadness of losing her mother as a young child.

She felt a connection to this boy, not just because of her own sense of loss but because she felt responsible to deliver the letter addressed to him.

'It's a real mystery then,' said Chelsea. 'But this isn't helping you. We should look at all the Randall's in the phone book and call them. That would be a start.'

The two women pored over the telephone book. After several hours of phoning they were no nearer answers. They began by ringing the M. Randalls and then all the Randalls in the metropolitan area, noting down the responses as they went.

'Why couldn't the name be Radinisky or something like that,' moaned Chelsea when they took a break near eight o'clock. 'There are far too many Randalls in this directory.'

'We'll have to stop soon. We can't phone after nine o'clock, it's bad manners.'

'It is obvious you're an accountant's daughter. You have so many rules, not to mention your compulsive list making.'

'You're right,' giggled Leisa, looking down at her immaculate writing and comparing it to Chelsea's method. Chelsea had put a cross beside those she had phoned and a thick red line through those who were dead ends. Leisa had circles and squiggles and arrows in a code that only she could decipher.

'When did you learn hieroglyphics, Leisa? When you floated down the Nile?' teased Chelsea.

'I understand my own system. You'd rip the pages out of the phone book if I let you.'

'I still don't know why I shouldn't,' said Chelsea pretending to reach for the huge directory.

'Oh, no you don't! It's time for another coffee break anyway.'

It was exactly eight fifty two when their search paid off. Leisa had just given her spiel—'I am phoning to locate a Michael Randall who may have had a connection to an Eleanor Mansfield.'

'I believe you have found who you are looking for,' a gentle woman's voice answered. 'Who may I ask is calling?'

Leisa told the woman her name and the brief circumstances of what she knew about Eleanor and scribbled down the address of the woman on the phone—14 Chelmsford Court, Shellharbour. A piece of the puzzle had fallen into place.

'What did she sound like?' quizzed Chelsea in excitement. 'What did she say?'

'She didn't say much at all really. But she didn't seem to think there was any mistake. She said she felt sure the photo was of her son. Her voice was cultured and she sounded quite calm. She seemed reserved. At least Shellharbour is only an hour south of Sydney. She said she could only see me between ten o'clock and midday. I guess she wants to be sure her son is at school. She probably doesn't want him upset. I'm glad she can see me tomorrow. I can't wait to deliver this; it's burning a hole in my conscience.'

Leisa looked at the photo of the boy. He was a robust beautiful child with the kind of ruddy complexion that comes from outdoor living. His hands were thrust in his pockets and his chestnut hair was unruly. She looked up at Chelsea.

'I just hope that this doesn't upset the little boy in the photo— he looks a real sweetheart,' said Leisa softly.

Author

Linda was born and raised in a small country town on the east coast of Australia, near Lake Macquarie. She has two sons who think their only job in life is to keep both her feet on the ground. She is addicted to sunshine, large bodies of water and living life to the full. She gained the attention of a publisher when her short stories found critical acclaim on the ABC website, 'The Making of Modern Australia'.

Linda's characters have resilience and warmth and her books are enriched by wit, spirit and surprise. She attributes this mix to her Irish/British convict heritage. Sharp observation is crafted with depth and compassion, as she explores the human experience with fearless candour. Many of her books feature her skill as an artist.

Other Published Titles by Linda Brooks:

Nonfiction:
An Australian Childhood

Poetry:

Adult fiction:
Behind Whispering Hands
The Unprize
A broken hallelujah
Scarlett doesn't live here anymore
Under the Bracken Fern

Children's books:
A Tabby Never Forgets
An Angels Tears
Callan the Chameleon (Asperger's Syndrome)
Dusty Bunny's Very Important Job
Ethereal Land
Izzy & Pudding the Cat
I want a monkey!
Madam Iris Bigglesworth
The Frog that Hiccupped
When the stars move
Who Stole Christmas?

Publisher of the anthologies:
We are Australian'
The Great Australian Shed
Waltzing Matilda

Linda Brooks